KV-198-532

Upon his retirement, Edward Hewitt at last saw the opportunity to realise the ambition of a lifetime.

The first volumes of The Cartwright Saga, *Where Waters Meet and The Harbinger of Doom*, were greeted with great acclaim.

The second volume — *The Miller's Daughters*, was equally successful.

RETURN TO WATERSMEET
Final Part of the Cartwright Saga

The appearance of a certain young man within the Cartwright family circle, and the advent of the Second World War, almost devastated the well-known Hull-based shipbuilding firm. The city of Kingston-upon-Hull suffered horrendous losses through the indiscriminate bombing of the city during the war, including hundreds of lives, shops, churches, factories, and thousands of houses. Also, the majority of the whole dock area was completely destroyed. Yet the people never gave in, and their great city rose like a Phoenix from the ashes.

Books by Edward Hewitt
Published by The House of Ulverscroft:

THE CARTWRIGHT SAGA:
WHERE WATERS MEET VOL 1
HARBINGER OF DOOM VOL 2
THE MILLER'S DAUGHTERS VOL 3
EMMA VOL 4

LATENT VISION

EDWARD HEWITT

RETURN TO WATERSMEET

The Cartwright Saga
Volume Five (Final Part)

Complete and Unabridged

ULVERSCROFT
Leicester

First published in Great Britain

First Large Print Edition
published 2001

The moral right of the author has been asserted

British Library CIP Data

Hewitt, Edward
    Return to Watersmeet.—Large print ed.—
(The Cartwright saga)
Ulverscroft large print series: romance
1. Love stories
2. Large type books
I. Title
823.9'14 [F]

ISBN 0–7089–4417–5

Published by
F. A. Thorpe (Publishing)
Anstey, Leicestershire

Set by Words & Graphics Ltd.
Anstey, Leicestershire
Printed and bound in Great Britain by
T. J. International Ltd., Padstow, Cornwall

This book is printed on acid-free paper

Prologue

Since the death of James, his only remaining son and heir, in that terrible car accident, Charles Cartwright had been unable to concentrate on any kind of work at the shipyard, for he could see no future for the Cartwright family name.

Because of her husband's abnormal lethargic attitude, Rose had a long discussion with their doctor, and he had suggested, the two of them should embark on an extended cruise, possibly to Egypt and down the Nile, spending some time seeing the sights, such as the Pyramids and the Valley of the Kings.

With very little effort Rose had succeeded in persuading Charles to go along with the doctor's suggestion, and some three months later, they had returned, both of them sporting an enviable sun tan, and simply exuding health and vitality.

When Charles eventually returned to work on the morning following their return, he was both amazed and very pleasantly surprised, at

1

the efficient way Paul had succeeded in the running of the yard, during his absence. So much so in fact, that he mentioned it to Rose after dinner that night, and she quietly reminded him of what Emma had once said. 'That Uncle Charles still had one son. Paul!'

At the time Charles was so consumed with grief, that he would have none of it, and refused to discuss the matter further. However, 'Time being the great Healer' she undoubtedly is, and particularly since his visit to the yard that day, he was now prepared to look more favourably upon his illegitimate offspring, and accede to his wife's wishes, having Paul Hunt, change his name by deed poll to, Paul Cartwright!

Paul, who had never forgiven his mother for the disparaging remarks she had made to Emma, about her and Charlotte her mother, that first day he had taken Emma home, had acquiesced immediately to the changing of his name, and had since moved in to live permanently at Mount Pleasant, where he was treated as the son and heir of Charles Cartwright.

1

One month before Emma, the love child of Tom Laceby and the late, beautiful unpredictable Charlotte, was due to return home from the Finishing School For Young Ladies in Switzerland, Paul had proposed to her on the telephone. Of course she had immediately accepted, and consequently by the time she arrived, all the arrangements were well under way to making this wedding, one of the social high points of the year.

As Emma alighted from the train at Paragon Station, an excited, ebullient Paul was waiting for her, with a porter standing beside him to attend to the luggage.

Paul took her in his arms, kissed and hugged her. 'Darling, you look marvellous,' he greeted her.

She reciprocated, kiss for kiss, then replied demurely. 'I hardly think so Paul. I have been travelling for hours and hours in that noisy smelly old train. I feel grubby and tired, and all I need at the moment, is a long soak in a lovely hot bath.'

Taking her by the hand, Paul led Emma along the platform, through the ticket office, and outside to the waiting Rolls. It was there, that the ex aristocrat, the once famous Lady Emma Brackley, now just plain Emma Laceby, though certainly not in looks, received one of the most violent shocks of her young life.

The smart uniformed chauffeur was standing with his back to them, just stacking the last of her cases into the car boot, then he closed the lid and turned. She felt her face drain of all colour, as she blanched totally white, faltered and almost fainted. For this man who had brought her husband to be, to meet her off the train, was the same man to whom she had willingly lost her virginity, some three years ago, in her father's log cabin, in the middle of Brackley's wood! *None other than ERIC TEESDALE!!*

Fortunately, Paul had moved to the other side of the car, as Eric opened the rear door for her. His face remained a mask, completely devoid of any sign of recognition, for which Emma was very thankful. As she sat back in the luxurious interior of the big car, Paul turned to her, put his arm around her shoulders, and drew her close, intending to kiss her.

'My darling, I have waited so long for this mo-,' he broke off in mid-sentence. 'Whatever's the matter darling? You're as white as a sheet. Please tell me what's wrong.'

Emma lowered her eyes before his ardent gaze. How could she tell her future husband, that the man he employed as his chauffeur, was the same man she had asked to take her to her father's cabin, and had then seduced him!

So Emma, being the daughter of Charlotte, and still retaining a strong unforgettable strain of her mother's waywardness, blandly told the first lie, in this long awaited reunion. 'Paul dear, nothing is wrong. If I appear as you say, then I suppose the reason is because I've had such an intolerable journey, and a terribly long day.'

'Of course my darling, how thoughtless of me, I'm awfully sorry, I really should have known better than to expect you to fall into my arms immediately, after all this time.'

Emma relaxed, closed her eyes and lay her head upon his shoulder, as the car moved smoothly and silently forward. When she first recognized Eric Teesdale, her mind had an instant flashback to that wonderful day, three years ago, to the small log cabin in that beautiful idyllic woodland setting. To the hard muscular body of this man, with whom she had lain naked, on the same bed Tom Laceby had shared with her ravishing seductive mother Charlotte!

5

Now, as the movement of the car lulled Emma's senses, she allowed herself to relive that day again. Once more she experienced the sudden sharp pain, and then the utter exquisite joy of that first union with a man. Emma felt the hot blood surging through her veins, and as her vivid imagination ran riot, she clenched her small fists to prevent herself crying out in her ecstasy.

Paul turned to her, he was surprised at the colour of her complexion. 'You appear much better now my darling, your cheeks are quite flushed. Do you feel all right?'

He had sounded far away, then suddenly realising where she was, Emma came back to earth with a bump. 'What? Er, yes thank you dear. I do feel rather warm though, may we have a window open please?'

Her fiancé, suspecting nothing untoward, carried out her request. 'Of course you may,' he replied, as he turned back to her, and taking both her hands in his, he gently squeezed them.

At that precise moment, Emma caught Eric Teesdale watching her in his rear view mirror, and still holding his gaze, for some inexplicable reason, she snatched her hands away from the grasp of her husband to be!

A bewildered Paul stared at her, with hurt and consternation in his eyes, yet he just sat back and said nothing.

Emma was immediately contrite. 'Darling Paul, please forgive me. I have no idea why I did that stupid thing,' she cooed, stroking his cheek and kissing his ear. 'You see I have only been living with young ladies for the past three years, and have completely forgotten how to behave correctly in male company.'

However, Emma conveniently omitted to mention the fact, that her and two other friends, regularly left the Finishing School For Young Ladies every week-end, and indulged in extremely erotic sexual shenanigans, in a house belonging to one of three men, with whom they had become acquainted!

As the car pulled into the driveway leading to Mount Pleasant, Emma thrilled once again to the sight of that huge glorious dome dominating the entire house.

'At least some things never change,' she whispered, almost to herself.

Eric drew up at the foot of the steps leading to the main entrance. 'Why have we stopped here Paul?' she asked, surprise in her voice.

He smiled. 'I thought you would like to say hello to your Aunt Rose, and possibly Uncle Charles if he's at home, before going along to your father's cottage.'

Emma stepped out, as the chauffeur held

the car door open for her. 'Thank you Eric,' she said politely.

Paul frowned. 'You're being rather familiar with the staff darling. Anyway, how do you know his name is Eric?'

'Oh! Darling, don't be so stuffy,' she replied, with a chuckle. 'I knew Eric Teesdale, long before I ever met you. He used to be the head groom at Brackley Hall. I've known him all my life.'

In later life, Paul Cartwright would remember that remark made by his beautiful wife to be, he would remember it and ponder upon it.

Her aunt came down the steps to meet her. 'Hello Emma darling, it is so lovely to see you home safe and sound. Did you have a pleasant journey? And how are you my dear? Ready for the wedding?'

Emma returned the kiss and the hug. She loved her Aunt Rose, it would have been very difficult not to, for she was so sweet and kind. So very different from her sister Charlotte, Emma thought poignantly, as she tried to remember what her late beautiful, utterly unpredictable mother, was really like.

Paul interrupted her reverie. 'Darling, your aunt was speaking to you, and asked if you had a pleasant journey.'

She turned to Rose. 'Terribly sorry Aunt

Rose, just for a moment there, I was reminiscing. I was thinking of my mother, and wondering what she would have thought of me now. Yes, I had a very pleasant journey, and I'm very well thank you. Also, I think I'm almost ready for the wedding,' she added, with a radiant smile.

Rose squeezed her hand. 'I'm sure Charlotte would be very proud of you, if she could see you today, my dear,' she remarked quietly. 'Now come along indoors, and tell me all about your wonderful life.'

They mounted the steps together, with Paul following in their wake.

'Isn't Uncle Charles at home today aunt?' Emma asked, when they were seated in the drawing room, replete with the ubiquitous cups of tea and buttered scones.

'No my dear. I'm afraid he had rather an important meeting at City Hall, something to do with the building of communal air raid shelters, within the city limits.'

Emma looked startled. 'Communal air raid shelters? Within the city limits. What on earth for aunt?'

Paul stepped in. 'Well you see my dear, things have moved on a bit since you were last home, and the Germans are getting restive again. You must have heard about the spectre of war, and the war drums beating out across Europe, even in Switzerland?'

'No Paul, I haven't. We were in rather a quiet backwater you know. However, now I come to think of it, I did notice rather an unusually large number of German soldiers standing about on station platforms, as our train passed through, though at the time I thought nothing of it, I just surmised the Germans were playing their silly war games again.'

Paul appeared serious. 'I'm afraid not my darling. I know one thing, I'm very pleased you are here on this side of the English Channel!'

Emma chuckled. 'Paul darling, I hope the Germans are not the only reason you are pleased I'm home.'

'No of course not,' he replied, catching her mood, and smiling with her. 'Just one of many.'

Rose summoned the maid to clear away the tea things. 'I think you should be going now darling, to see your father and Milly,' she said, turning to her niece. 'Though of course Tom may be out, somewhere on the estate, but Milly should be at home.'

After a brief hug and kiss, Emma walked out to the waiting Rolls, with Paul in close attendance. The cottage looked charming in the late afternoon sun, on this beautiful autumnal day, and as the car stopped, an excited Milly rushed out to greet her beloved Emma.

'Oh! My darling, you look marvellous,' she gushed. 'Not a day older than when you left three years ago.'

★ ★ ★

Eric was struggling to lift the largest of her three cases from the car boot, and she moved to help him, as Paul and Milly carried the other two inside.

They were very close now, and as they grappled with the heavy case. 'Where are you living Eric? she asked, in a fierce whisper.

Eric dropped his end of the case, as he stared at her. However, fortunately he quickly recovered. 'In a flat over the garage,' he replied in similar vein. 'Why?

Emma covered his hand with her own, and pressed hard. 'Because I need to see you of course, you must know why. When is a good time?'

'If you can get out of going to church with all the others, tomorrow morning, when I return with the Rolls.'

'That's better Eric, I think we have it now,' said Emma in her normal voice, as Paul and Milly returned.

Milly escorted Emma to her room. 'Now tell me all about your wonderful experiences while you have been away from home, and all the men you have met along the way,' she said, as Emma flopped down upon the soft feather bed.

Emma laughed, a happy carefree kind of laugh. 'Oh! Milly darling, I couldn't possibly tell you about them all, I'm afraid there isn't time, not now. We shall have to start first thing in a morning. Anyway forget my wanderings for a moment. How the devil does Eric Teesdale come to be working here?'

★ ★ ★

Milly's expression changed. 'I don't really know,' she replied quietly. 'I think it has something to do with that fight he had with Sir Michael, over you and the fact that Charlotte was your mother, and Tom your father. If you remember it was Eric who followed them into Brackley's Wood, then reported back to Sir Richard, and all I can think, is that somehow Michael found out, and that is why they had a fight. Anyway, soon afterwards apparently Eric handed in his notice and left, he later applied for the job here as head groom, and was accepted.'

Emma's smooth brow was creased in deep

thought for a moment, then she looked at her companion. 'Yes, I know all that is true, but I still fail to understand, how he came to be taken on here. I mean, presumably he would have to be interviewed by my father, and I can't believe he would be inclined to forgive and forget quite so easily, or so quickly. For after all, it was because of Eric Teesdale, that daddy lost his job in the first place, and anyway, didn't he think I should be embarrassed, when I eventually arrived home, and found Eric working here?'

Milly gazed upon her young friend, and thought how beautiful she was, the time she had spent abroad, had given her an extra air of confidence, and the years had given her a fuller figure, which seemed to have increased her allure. Even so, she didn't seem to have learnt much about men!

At last Milly spoke. 'My dearest Emma, all Tom would be thinking about, was what a good man Eric was with horses. I'm sorry to disappoint you darling, but I don't suppose any other thought ever entered his head. And at the time we were desperately in need of a head groom.'

At that moment a voice boomed up from below. 'Hello there! Is anyone at home?'

Emma leapt off the bed, and literally flew

downstairs, taking the last three steps in one jump, right into her father's arms. 'Oh! Daddy,' she cried, with tears streaming unchecked down her cheeks. 'How wonderful to be home with you at last. I have missed you so dreadfully. I thought this day would never come.'

Tom held her vibrant young body close for a long moment, kissed her upon the cheek, and tasted her salt laden tears, then gently eased her away, and holding her at arm's length, he looked into her lovely eyes, and a lump arose in his throat, as he saw once again. *His beautiful Charlotte!*

'What is it daddy? What's wrong?', she asked apprehensively, as she saw his expression change, and his face pale.

'Oh! Emma!' he whispered, as he clung to her, and held her tightly, once again.

'What's the matter daddy. Have I done something to upset you?'

He fought for his self control, and at last appeared much calmer. 'No kitten, you have done nothing wrong. It's just that, when I looked into your eyes a moment ago, *I saw your mother, as plainly as I see you now!*'

His daughter smiled through her tears, a loving tender smile. 'But daddy, that is the most wonderful thing to have happened, I know it is. This must be some kind of sign to let us know that mummy is safe and happy, wherever she is!'

Tom moved into the room, and taking his daughter with him, he sat down in an easy chair, and drew her down upon his knee, then trying to lift the conversation from this melancholy trough, to which he had inadvertently allowed it to sink, he held her hands in his, and marvelled once again, as he gazed upon her beauty, and wondered for the thousandth time, how such a stunning ravishing girl, could have been conceived in sin, in an old log cabin, in the middle of Brackley's Wood!

He smiled. 'Yes that may be so my darling. However, let us talk now of the present. Are you pleased to be home?'

'Why yes of course daddy,' she replied, much relieved that he seemed more relaxed.

'Good, and are you looking forward to your wedding with young Paul Cartwright?'

'Again, yes of course daddy. Are you looking forward to giving me away?' she asked capriciously.

'No, you know perfectly well I'm not. I only wish Charlotte could have been here to see you walk down the aisle. That would have made a perfect day complete. Sorry Emma, I didn't mean to go down that road again,' he added quickly, as he saw the light fade from her eyes.

'I only hope young Cartwright knows and appreciates what a wonderful wife he's getting, that's all.'

2

However, the only time Emma was able to see Eric on that Sunday morning, was when he came to collect her in the Rolls, for Tom, Milly and Paul insisted she accompany them to church, because Rose and Charles had invited all four to Mount Pleasant for the Sunday Roast, when they returned.

There were several members of the elderly population, who could well remember the exploits of the legendary Thomas Cartwright, and though he had been looked upon as the fountain of integrity and honour among men, of late a few had begun to doubt that assumption. For a number of these gentlemen made certain innuendoes, and cast aspersions upon the validity of such statements about the character of Thomas.

Some had even been heard to say, that Thomas Cartwright had sown his seed in another bed, apart from those he had shared with his wife, the elegant Kate Earnshaw, and his beautiful sensuous, Italian looking mistress Maria!

The reasons for these unfounded insinuations, was a strapping young man of some twenty four years, an almost exact clone of the late Thomas Cartwright! It has been known throughout history, for a gene in a stronger personality, to appear several generations later, and though he stood four inches shorter than his supposed forbear, and lacked the colossal strength for which Thomas had been noted, apparently this is what had happened in the case of Tim Carter. Even his initials were the same!

Tim appeared very much like a young Thomas, he possessed the same head of blonde curly hair, which for so many years had been the secret pride and joy of Thomas, until the loss of his wife and family in that terrible act of revenge by the banks of the River Humber, below the village of Watersmeet, had overnight, turned his golden locks to silver!

Charles, whilst interviewing an assortment of young budding apprentice shipwrights at Trinity College, with a view to giving the best of them employment in his workforce, was the first to notice the striking similarity between this tall young man, and his own late grandfather. The consequence of that interview, was that Tim Carter had been accepted as a draughtsman, in the offices of Earnshaw & Cartwright, Shipbuilders, in the City of Kingston-upon-Hull.

All of this had taken place some ten years ago, and during that time, particularly after the shattering loss of his son James, Charles had grown quite close to Tim Carter. So much so, he had invited Tim to spend the week-end at Mount Pleasant, and though he had said nothing to Rose of his plan, he was hoping his daughter Marcia, and the good-looking Tim, may be attracted to each other.

★   ★   ★

Marcia, the only daughter of Charles and Rose, who had for so many years, remained quietly in the background, and seemed immune to everything that happened around her, like an island of calm, washed by a turbulent sea, had recently and very suddenly, appeared to have grown up, into a completely changed and very attractive young lady.

For though she could easily have stayed at home, and led an utterly useless life as a young lady of leisure, then eventually married some son of a member of the local landed gentry, such an option had never been a part of Marcia's nature. Since early childhood, she had always loved playing at being a nurse, and after leaving college, had immediately taken up that wonderful, yet very arduous profession, and was now living in nurse's accommodation, within the grounds of one of the local hospitals in the city, completely dedicated to her calling.

Marcia had now attained the age of almost twenty three years, and being of such a lovely sunny nature, was very popular with her patients and her contemporaries, particularly the male members, one of whom was a doctor named Ralph Skinner, and though he wasn't very well liked by many members of staff at the hospital, he always seemed to go out of his way to please Marcia.

Dr. Skinner was in his early thirties, and though still unmarried, had during his lifetime, embarked upon several affairs, generally with young, pretty nurses.

★   ★   ★

However, being of such a mercenary nature, and forever on the prowl for a young lady with an impeccable family background, and wealthy parents, all his previous forages into the realms of the fair sex, had ended in complete disaster, sometimes even violence! And now he was chasing the beautiful, talented, gentle daughter of Charles Cartwright, for he couldn't believe his luck, when he discovered who her parents were, where they lived, and what they owned!

However, unknown to the good doctor, or to Marcia, another young man, far more predatory than Ralph Skinner, was about to be introduced into their quiet lives. A young man who would cause much intrigue, consternation and heart ache, to the Cartwright family!

On that Sunday afternoon, a fly appeared in the ointment of Charles' well planned conspiracy, in the shape of Ralph Skinner! Charles had met the man previously, and was not particularly enamoured by his nature. He was the very reason he had invited Tim, to try and persuade Marcia to forget that Dr. Skinner ever existed!

Ralph and Marcia were outside on the drive, where he was showing off his latest acquisition, namely a flashy brand new, red M.G. sports car, when suddenly, with a great deal of noise, Tim shuddered to a halt, in an old Ford Pop, creating massive clouds of dust, which rather unfortunately completely enveloped the two of them, and Ralph's shiny new car!

Tim had his window down, and before he could alight from the car, Ralph Skinner, coughing and spluttering, was suddenly shown in his true colours.

'What the hell do you think you're doing, you bloody moron? You have completely covered my new car, my friend and I in dust, that old heap of scrap should not be allowed on the road, and certainly should not be allowed to park anywhere near this car of mine. Now get out, and I'll damn well thrash you!'

Charles, who was standing on the top step of the entrance to Mount Pleasant, had overheard this diatribe, and smiled quietly to himself, whilst Marcia disgusted by the arrogant attitude of her guest, stood rooted to the spot, and awaited with bated breath the reaction of this rather good looking young stranger.

Very slowly, and with stylish nonchalance, Tim Carter allowed two long legs to emerge from the low seat of his car, these were then followed by the rest of him, and as more of this tall handsome young man appeared, the further the lower jaw of Dr.Skinner dropped, and the further he backed away.

Finally Tim was out of the car, and as he stood towering above the hapless doctor, he leaned forward, and grabbing Ralph by his shirt front, lifted him so that his eyes were on a level with his own. 'What was that you called me mister? No, don't bother to answer, though I can assure you, where I come from, we are not in the habit of swearing in front of our womenfolk.'

The words were spoken in no more than a sibilant whisper, and yet strangely, they carried easily to the ears of Charles and his lovely daughter.

As Tim released his hold of the man's shirt, he was so terrified, he fell to the ground, and still upon his hands and knees, he spoke tremulously, and made the most bizarre statement. 'I am not a mister, I'm a doctor.'

Tim, before turning contemptuously away, chuckled aloud, and replied. 'Well, let's hope your bedside manners, are much better than any you have displayed so far.' It was then he saw Charles standing in the shadow of the entrance to the house, and as previously instructed, when meeting socially, he addressed him by his first name. 'Hello Charles,' he boomed. 'Lovely day. Some of your guests are inclined to get a bit uppity! Wherever did you find that one?'

Inwardly Ralph Skinner was heaping all kinds of curses upon the head of this usurper, for he was well aware of his own limitations, and knew he would have no chance to ingratiate himself further, in the affections of the very desirable Marcia, if this tall stranger proved to be a competitor for her hand.

Meanwhile, Charles had thoroughly enjoyed

the discomfort and embarrassment, heaped upon Ralph, especially in front of Marcia. His little scheme couldn't have started better, and he silently congratulated himself, upon this ploy of inviting Tim here to help distract his lovely daughter, and steer her away from the mercenary conniving doctor, whom he thought, was too old for her anyway.

It was unfortunate therefore, that Charles Cartwright hadn't bothered to learn more about the private life of Tim Carter. For he had rather an unenviable reputation of being very much a ladies man, and though extremely likable, and possessing terrific charisma, he was really rather a raffish rogue, and had already laid waste, several of the young girl's lives he had touched, during the comparatively short time he had spent in this world as an adult! Had Charles taken the trouble to discover more about Tim, it is highly unlikely he would have been invited to Mount Pleasant on that particular week-end, for the sole purpose of distracting the stunningly beautiful, yet very vulnerable Marcia, away from the unwanted advances of Dr.Ralph Skinner.

As Ralph staggered to his feet, he moved towards the object of his affections, endeavouring to produce a rather sickly smile. 'I'm awfully sorry about that little debacle my dear. Isn't that person really an ignorant lout?'

Apparently Marcia didn't seem to think so, for she completely ignored her former escort, as she walked past him and went to her father. 'Father, where have you been hiding this handsome young man?' she trilled, as Tim joined them, and gazed with blatant admiration upon the countenance and figure of this lovely young woman.

'Sorry my dear, I haven't been hiding him, though even you must agree, that would be rather difficult, considering his size. Marcia, meet Tim Carter, one of my staff from the shipyard,' then turning to the young man. 'Tim, may I introduce my one and only daughter, Marcia.'

'You certainly may sir,' replied Tim eagerly, as the two young people shook hands, and Marcia demurely murmured a quiet. 'Pleased to make your acquaintance, Mr. Carter.'

Tim chuckled. 'No, Miss Marcia, please call me Tim. By the way, I hope I didn't break up any long standing friendship just now, between you and that rather irate elderly looking gentleman, standing over there by his car, did I?'

Marcia lifted her fingers to her mouth, and though she was smiling, tried to sound serious. 'Hush Tim, he will hear you, and he

25

will definitely not like being called an elderly gentleman. Apart from that, he is a doctor and I'm a nurse, and we both work at the same hospital. So you see it really wouldn't do any good for my career if I crossed him, for he is after all, a very clever doctor, and highly thought of by his peers, though not by any members of the female staff I'm afraid.'

'Oh! Why not? Does he fancy himself as a bit of a Casanova?' asked Tim, in some surprise. 'Because if so, I can't imagine why.'

Marcia laughed aloud. 'Tim you really shouldn't mock the afflicted, it's not his fault if he isn't as well endowed as you,' then suddenly realising what she had said, she blushed prettily, and endeavoured to put matters right. 'Don't you dare say anything Tim Carter! You know perfectly well, I meant in looks and physique.'

Tim smiled, obviously enjoying this first encounter with his employer's beautiful daughter, yet being painfully aware that Charles was hovering nearby. Consequently, not wishing to give any wrong impression about his true nature, or any indication of how much he fancied Marcia, he replied quietly. 'I would never have thought otherwise. Whatever you meant Marcia, I fully intend to take it as a compliment!'

Though Marcia breathed a sigh of relief,

and returned Tim's smile, she still wasn't quite sure that he was being completely truthful.

At that moment Paul and Emma came out of the house and joined the group, and were then duly introduced to Dr.Skinner and Tim Carter.

'I have had a brilliant idea,' gushed Emma, as she looked around at her new found friends, allowing her gaze to linger just that moment longer than was necessary, in the direction of Tim! 'It is such a lovely afternoon, let's make a foursome for a game of tennis. What do you think?'

Everyone was in agreement, with the exception of Paul. 'Terribly sorry darling,' he said, addressing his future bride. 'There is something I must attend to at the yard this afternoon. However, there are still four of you, so off you go and enjoy your game, then I will try and join you later.'

'But Paul,' Emma protested, 'Dash it all, it is Sunday, and also only my second day at home. Surely you don't have to go in today?'

'Sorry Emma, I'm afraid I must,' he replied over his shoulder, as he walked away.

There was silence for a moment after he had gone, though if it had been possible, the others would have heard the brain of Tim Carter working overtime. For it wasn't very often he had the choice of two such stunningly beautiful partners!

'Very well girls,' he said, smiling in the direction of Emma. For having weighed up all the options, Tim had decided to make a play for Emma, he thought she appeared to be the most likely of the two girls, to respond to his advances. And of course he could return to Marcia at any time, if this little flirtation failed! 'Let's play tennis. I will partner Emma, and you Dr.Skinner, partner Marcia. Is that all right?'

Ralph Skinner readily agreed, for of course Marcia was the young lady he was interested in, she was the only reason for his being here at Mount Pleasant, on this lovely autumnal afternoon.

It quickly became obvious right from the start of the match, who was going to win, for neither Emma or Tim had anything like the ability and flair for the game that Marcia and her doctor friend possessed.

After only half-an-hour, a highly embarrassed, belittled and very much outplayed Tim Carter decided he'd had enough. 'I'm sorry Emma,' he panted. 'But I seem to be a little out of practice. Can we call it a day?'

Emma, who had been playing her heart out, and doing her best to retain some form of dignity on the court, was astounded at the sheer incompetence of one who, on the surface at least, appeared to have all the necessary attributes of an excellent athlete, yet was so obviously out of condition. Of course Emma had no knowledge of the private lifestyle, the late night drinking parties, or of the many women who shared the life of her tennis partner, some of whom were of very doubtful repute!

'Yes I suppose so, if you wish,' she replied coolly, though actually she was very hot, and perspiring freely from her exertions. Then turning to the other couple. 'I'm terribly sorry Ralph, Marcia, but my partner doesn't seem to be quite as fit as he appears.'

The cool unruffled, immaculate Ralph Skinner laughed aloud, enjoying immensely, this moment of unexpected triumph. 'I say Carter, perhaps you should consult your doctor,' he chortled gleefully. 'He may be able to help.'

A disconsolate Tim turned miserably away, angry with himself for playing badly, just when he had so desperately wanted to make a good impression on the beautiful, very desirable Emma. However, his angry mood changed immediately Emma spoke.

'I say Tim,' her voice had changed, and was almost a caress. 'I feel terribly hot after all that exercise during the game, and Uncle

Charles has provided hot and cold showers in the changing rooms. Shall we indulge?'

They were very close, her moist parted lips, and the look in her beautiful eyes, were a blatant invitation, and one which Tim had no intention of refusing. 'Certainly my dear,' he replied, as he felt his pulses quicken, and the old juices begin to flow.

That day, the beautiful illegitimate daughter of a surreptitious liaison between Tom Laceby, and Charlotte, the late wayward Lady Brackley, was once again transported to those wonderful heights of sexual satisfaction, which she had first experienced in her father's log cabin, and had then continued during her stay at The College For Young Ladies, in Switzerland, and to which she had virtually become addicted, almost as to a powerful drug!

Tim Carter couldn't believe his luck, in meeting such a beautiful, passionate young woman, and one who, for the first time in his highly flirtatious, womanising career, had actually been able to teach him, some of the many and varied ways of making love!

Afterwards, they had taken a cold shower together to try to cool their ardour, even so it seemed utterly impossible for the lovely irrepressible Emma, to keep her hands off her handsome new friend.

'When can I see you again?', she asked, rubbing her flawless naked skin vigorously, until it glowed with the health of youth.

'As soon as possible,' Tim replied, blatantly admiring her beautiful body, whilst trying to share part of the huge white bath towel, in an effort to dry himself.

'Find your own towel,' laughingly cried Emma, as she ran from the shower room on to the veranda, with Tim in hot pursuit.

They halted abruptly, for Marcia, Dr.Ralph Skinner and Milly were just walking past the bottom of the steps, leading from the courts to the showers!

Milly gave a vociferous, shocked *'EMMA!'* However, before she could add anything further, the recalcitrant bride to be, had whirled around and bolted back to the shower room, with her lover in close attendance, leaving the three bemused onlookers in stunned silence, and apparently frozen to the spot.

As they regained their mobility and moved slowly forward, Ralph edged a little closer to Marcia. 'Well I should think that little episode takes care of your Tim Carter, my dear,' he remarked silkily, with a smirk upon his not too handsome mouth. It was at that moment, Ralph Skinner discovered he had made a very bad mistake.

Marcia had been more hurt by what had just transpired, than she would ever admit to anyone, even to herself, and she turned on poor Ralph, like a veritable she-devil. 'Allow me to inform you Dr.Skinner, that naked person you just saw cavorting with the whore, who is shortly to become my sister-in-law, is not, repeat not, my Tim Carter, nor does any of this revealing, disgusting charade, give you the right to address me as Your Dear! Everyone at the hospital knows how you have treated your past lovers! So please run along, get in your bloody car, and get off my father's property, and don't bother coming back. Ever!'

Each word was like a barb, dripping with vitriol, and Ralph blanched as this angelic looking young woman tore into him, exposing him as no other had ever dared, and without a word, Dr.Ralph Skinner turned on his heel, and left the field of battle, utterly defeated.

3

Marcia returned to her room at Mount Pleasant, while a very angry and rather distraught Milly, strode around the confines of Tom Laceby's cottage, impatiently awaiting the appearance of the promiscuous Emma. After glancing at the clock for the umpteenth time, Milly at last decided to go out and search for her, and just as she opened the door, a rather subdued looking Emma was walking down the garden path, towards her lifelong friend and companion.

No word passed between them as Milly held the door open for her to enter the cottage, but immediately it closed, she tore into Emma. 'What the hell do you think you're playing at young lady? Obviously you have no idea of Tim Carter's reputation, otherwise he would never have been allowed to lay a finger on you. I really can't imagine why you behaved so disgustingly, are you so bloody desperate, that you can't wait? Damn it all Emma, in case you have forgotten, you're getting married in three week's time, to probably the most eligible bachelor in the county.'

Slowly Emma turned to face her belligerent accuser, and that split second was frozen in the mind of Milly, for all time! For this wasn't Emma staring at her, even though she knew it was Emma standing before her. Oh! No, those eyes, just for that brief infinitesimal second, were the eyes of her late mother, and Milly's beloved *Charlotte!*

With a strangled sob, Milly lunged forward and enfolded the bemused, astonished Emma in her arms. For the message in those eyes had been touched with a poignant amalgam of accusation and pleading, and Emma fought back the tears, as she realised the trembling Milly was silently sobbing, as she held her in a tight embrace.

'Milly, what's wrong? please tell me. It isn't just the fact that you saw Tim and me naked. There's something else, isn't there?'

Gradually Milly calmed down and ceased her heart rending sobs. 'Yes darling, there is. Just now when I was telling you off, and you stared at me, I looked into your eyes, only they were not your eyes, they were Charlotte's, your late mother's, and in some strange way, I think she was trying to tell me not to be too harsh with you. It was only a very fleeting glimpse darling, and then in less time than a single heartbeat, it was gone.'

Milly's statement evoked a fresh wave of tears from the two women, and they flung themselves down upon the large sofa, united in their grief, for the loss of one who had played such a huge part in both their lives.

Eventually the heaving sobs subsided, and they became much calmer. 'I'm terribly sorry Milly, for all the trouble and uproar I've caused,' Emma began tentatively. 'You see, the trouble is, whenever I'm near a good looking man, I don't seem to be able to control myself, I think this is something I may have inherited from mummy. It's almost like a drug Milly, I used to try and fight it at first, but now I just go along with my feelings, and hope for the best!'

'I wish I'd had feelings like those, some twenty years ago,' said Milly dryly, though with a touch of sadness. 'I would have had a much better time!'

For the first time, since she had entered the cottage, Emma laughed, a lovely full throated chuckle. 'Oh! Darling Milly, you're a real tonic, I could never have coped here on my own, without you.' Then suddenly, this beautiful young woman, had a wonderful idea.

'Milly,' her voice was soft, almost a caress. 'It is never too late you know. You're not very old, you have years ahead yet. You could still feel like you wished you had, twenty years ago!'

Her companion stared at her askance. 'Darling, what on earth do you mean? What sly scheme are you plotting now?'

Emma bestowed upon her friend, her most brilliant smile, and then trying, quite unsuccessfully, to appear hurt, she replied. 'No sly scheme, dearest Milly,' she hesitated, but only momentarily, then after a slight cough, presumably to clear her throat of an imaginary blockage, she plunged on.

'You know more than anyone, how much I loved mummy, you also know how very much I love Tom Laceby, my father. Yet, though I had been home only a few short hours, I could tell immediately, how very lonely he is.'

Milly held up her hand. 'Stop right there young lady. What the devil are you trying to do, play matchmaker?' she asked, in an uncompromising tone.

Emma blushed slightly. 'And what if I am? You know I could never love you in the same way I loved mummy. However, you also know, that I do love you very much, and nothing would give me greater pleasure, than to see you and daddy united in marriage!'

Milly sat perfectly still, her mind trying to assimilate the outrageous words her companion had just uttered, and with her ego massaged beyond compare, she turned and faced this lovely girl, whom she had cared for, protected, and looked upon, almost as her own daughter, since the day Charlotte had brought her to Brackley Hall, all those years ago.

'Yes but,' Milly's voice was unnaturally high, she coughed and began again. 'Yes but Emma, supposing all you say is true, and Tom is lonely, which I imagine he is, because I know I am. What can I do to change the situation? I admit I could quite easily fall in love with him, he's a fine looking man, yet though we're living under the same roof, we may as well be miles apart.'

'I don't think that would be a very good idea!'

Though those few words had been softly spoken, they were sufficient to cause the two women to leap up off the sofa, and whirl around. Tom Laceby was leaning nonchalantly against a door jamb of the open doorway, a quiet smile upon his strong mouth.

'Daddy!' screamed Emma, as she rushed into his arms. 'How long have you been standing there? How much did you hear?' she asked, as Milly stood apprehensively by, waiting for him to reply, her colour high, and her heart pounding in her ears.

At last he spoke. 'Enough,' he said. 'At least, enough to show me what a fool I've been for the last three years! Why the devil didn't you come home earlier Emma, and bring Milly and I together?'

It was then he dropped his bombshell, as he turned and faced Milly. 'From a distance, I have learned to love and care for you over the years, but never dare say anything, because I didn't know how you would react, and I was afraid of losing you. However, what little I overheard of your conversation with Emma, has given me courage, and now I am brave enough to ask you something I have been wanting to ask for some considerable time.' Tom walked over to Milly, and took her hands in his. 'Milly, will you please marry me!'

Milly's reply was immediate, and surprisingly dramatic. 'Yes! Yes! Of course I will marry you Tom Laceby,' she cried, flinging herself into his open arms, as they indulged in a very passionate kiss, which even gave the watching Emma a slight twinge of envy.

Though as she looked upon this quite remarkable scene of the two people she loved most in the world, her lifelong friend and companion, and her father, locked together, in what could only be described as a lover's embrace, the tears began to flow freely down the satin smooth cheeks of this lovely girl, and not bothering to wipe them away, Emma rushed across the room and wrapped her arms around the happy couple.

'Oh! Daddy. Oh! Milly,' she sobbed, laughing and crying simultaneously. 'How wonderful. This is the best homecoming present, I could ever have had.' Suddenly, her crying stopped, as she dried her brimming eyes, and her countenance brightened. 'Daddy, Milly, I have just had the most brilliant idea. Let's have a double wedding!'

Flushed and breathless, the two broke apart. 'What?' they both asked together. Regaining a little of her normal composure, Milly continued. 'But darling, I have nothing to wear, not good enough for a wedding, well not for my wedding anyway.' She hesitated for a second, then her eyes shining, and her features glowing with a lovely smile, she continued. 'It really is a marvellous idea though, I'm sure you and I will be able to find something suitable, if we spend a day or two shopping.'

Once more Milly hesitated, then switching her gaze from Emma to Tom. 'Of course Emma, everything depends on what your father has to say, he may not want to get married on the same day as his daughter. I mean who will give you away, if we four are standing at the altar together?'

Tom smiled, as he reached out and again put his arm around the petite Milly. 'Don't you worry your pretty head about a small thing like that my dear,' and before he could continue, his lovely daughter cut in.

'And anyway, I have no intention of allowing one or two day's shopping to pass me by. Let's do it daddy, let us all get married together!' As she finished speaking, Emma moved towards the door.

'Where are you going darling?' her father asked. She turned and smiled. 'I'm just going to run along and tell Aunt Rose and Uncle Charles the wonderful news. May I?'

Tom returned the smile. 'Yes, but not on your own, Milly and I will come with you.'

So it was, a very happy threesome made their way to the front entrance of Mount Pleasant, and began mounting the steps, just as Paul opened the door, on his way to see Emma.

'Hello Paul,' they cried in unison.

'We three would like a word with you my darling,' continued Emma, as she deftly turned him around, then propelled him back through the already open door, into that huge hall, pausing only while Tom closed the door behind them.

'Now my lad,' began Emma, in a no

nonsense tone. 'We have some wonderful news, we were going to tell Aunt Rose and Uncle Charles, but now you are here, you may as well hear it first,' she paused, chiefly for effect, and apparently it worked.

Paul looked, first at one and then the other of his companions. 'Well I must say, this is bound to be good news, whatever it is. You all appear to have suddenly struck gold, or come into a small fortune. What is it? Tell me quickly for Heavens sake!'

They all laughed aloud at his impatience, and at that moment, Rose and Charles came out of the library, wondering what all the noise was about.

'Hello you four, what is all the fuss about?' began Charles. 'I must say you appear very happy and excited about something, except you Paul. Why aren't you joining in this bout of hilarity, and obvious happiness?'

'Because, Uncle Charles, he doesn't know what it's about,' chimed in Emma. 'We were on our way to tell you, when we met Paul at the entrance.'

'Tell them what?' shouted an irate Paul.

Emma rushed into the arms of her aunt. 'Oh! Aunt Rose, we have such wonderful news. You will never guess,' she cried, as she hugged and kissed her.

Paul stepped forward, and dragged her

away, then obviously fighting for self control, for by now his patience was wearing thin. 'Emma!' he shouted. Then in a more subdued tone. 'Will you please tell us, what the devil this is all about?'

Emma eased herself from his grip, and allowed her lovely eyes to wash over him. 'Yes my darling. I will tell you. We are getting married.'

His face was a picture of disbelief. 'I know that you idiot, we all know it!' He was shouting again.

However, fortunately for Paul, she let it pass, for today Emma was too happy to allow a small thing like being called an idiot, to spoil everything. 'Yes Paul darling,' she purred, I know you know that, but what you don't know. *Is that my beloved father and my dear sweet friend Milly, are going to be married on the same day we are!*'

For one split second, the silence was absolute, then everyone seemed to be talking at once. 'What?' shouted Charles. 'I say that's marvellous. Congratulations Tom,' he said, excitedly shaking the hand of his estate manager, while Rose wrapped her arms around Milly.

'Congratulations Milly, and you too Tom,' gushed Rose, as she kissed the future bride upon her cheek. 'Emma said your wedding is to be the same day as her and Paul. Oh! My dear, what a lot of work we have to do before then. However, don't you worry about it Milly, you will have a thousand and one things to do for yourself. Have you got a wedding dress yet? Also, if Tom is going to be standing beside you at the altar, who is going to give Emma away?'

'Now just calm down Rose,' chimed in her husband.

'You're more excited than Milly. I will give Emma away, if she will allow me to.'

Whatever Charles added to that statement, suddenly became lost in the mass of Emma's hair, as she rushed to him and thanked him profusely, whilst kissing him on both cheeks.

In the meantime Milly turned to Rose. 'No, I haven't a wedding dress as yet. Actually I only found out I was getting married, about twenty minutes ago! However, Emma and I are going into Hull on a shopping spree this week, so all being well, everything should be settled by next week-end.'

'I think we should all go along to the library, and have a drink to celebrate this wonderful piece of news,' said Charles, now he had finally managed to dislodge his over exuberant niece.

Everyone agreed in unison, and as they

made their way towards the door, Charles spoke to the butler, who a few minutes later knocked on the library door, and walked in with a bottle of Champagne.

The following morning, Emma had a word with her Uncle Charles, and the consequence of that, was Eric Teesdale drawing up in the Rolls, outside their cottage at ten-o-clock, to take her and Milly to Hull, for a glorious full day's shopping.

They each bought new clothes, including suits, dresses and hats. Then finally, in the very last shop, after almost giving up hope, Milly discovered her perfect wedding dress. They were both overjoyed with the result of their purchases, and could hardly contain themselves, until they arrived home, though of course neither Paul or Tom, were allowed so much as a glimpse of any wedding apparel.

Finally, the great day dawned, and as in the times of Thomas and Kate, Miles and Ruth, all the streets surrounding the church, were crammed with vehicles belonging to the many invited guests, and the pavements were packed with cheering boisterous crowds of expectant onlookers. For the fame of Cartwright's shipyard was known far and wide, so of course a wedding within the family circle, at once became a huge social occasion.

This wedding though, was of a very different nature, to any that had gone before. For this was a Double Wedding, and the number of guests far surpassed, any of the other Cartwright weddings. So much so in fact, a large marquee had been erected on the front lawns of Mount Pleasant, because the hall wasn't big enough to seat them all.

Fortunately the weather was very kind that day, and the church was packed, while crowds of disappointed folk, had to stand outside. However, they were all in good positions to enjoy the sight of the two happy couples, as they emerged from the church, into the sunshine of this lovely autumnal morning, while the church bells rang out their message of joy and hope, to all the people who had come to watch and listen, and to play their small part in this momentous occasion, on such a glorious day.

Paul and Emma in a white chauffeur driven Rolls Royce, led the huge convoy of cars from the church, through the city and along the country lanes, finally coming to a halt at the entrance to Mount Pleasant.

All the staff from the estate and the house, were lined up to greet the happy couple, which they did very vociferously, and as the final cheers died away, after alighting from the car, Paul scooped up his lovely bride, and carried her over the threshold into the house.

The whole procedure was repeated, as the second white Rolls stopped at the foot of the steps, and Tom Laceby, looking very smart in top hat and tails, helped his elegant bride out of the car.

One of Tom's friends, a foreman off the estate was his best man, while Paul, completely besotted and blindly in love with his beautiful bride, and not yet being aware of the frailties of human nature, or of Emma's promiscuous behaviour, had naively invited Tim Carter to carry out the duties of best man for him!

However, the weddings and the reception, including all the speeches were a huge success, particularly the catering, for cook and her minions, under the impeccable supervision of Rose, had served up a magnificent mouth watering feast of culinary delights, to suit all tastes of everyone present. When the frivolities and jollification were finally over, and the two happily married couples left the marquee to change into their honeymoon outfits, many of the guests drifted away and went to their cars, prior to driving away.

A few close friends however, those in the know, stayed a little longer, waiting for the return of the two brides and their grooms.

The clause which William Earnshaw had inserted into his contract with the railway company, when he sold them a certain strip of land, was still viable, and these few knew, that just after three-o-clock in the afternoon, the train which had recently left Paragon Station, heading for Doncaster, would halt at a certain place on the Cartwright estate, to collect two honeymoon couples! Just as that first very early steam contraption had stopped all those years ago, to pick up William and Lottie!

Because of their knowledge, the remaining company, several of whom were more than slightly inebriated, and amidst much singing and shouting, wandered down the drive, across the main road, and on towards the railway line, which ran alongside the River Humber. There they settled down to wait. Not for long though, before one of their members shouted. 'Here they come!'

Almost in the same second, someone else shouted. 'And here comes the train!'

Immediately the scene became utter chaos, enveloped in hissing steam, as the huge monster juddered and skidded to a stop, and everyone pushed and clamoured to get near the newlyweds to cover them with more confetti, and to shout advice, some of it quite lewd, most of it totally unnecessary, and to wish them bon voyage, as the huge wheels began to spin, then held, spun again, and eventually they gripped the shining metal rails, and the engine pulled majestically away, dragging the coaches behind it. And with windows down, much fluttering of handkerchiefs were visible, until the train rounded a bend, and all that remained was a trail of smoke, and the memory of that wonderful day.

For some inexplicable reason, silence had pervaded the small group of guests left standing by the side of the tracks, it seemed as if the main show was over now the chief actors had deserted the stage.

However, one certain young man who was present, did not intend an opportunity like this to pass him by. Tim Carter threw back his blonde head, and called in rather a loud voice. 'Come along folks cheer up, what you have just witnessed, doesn't have to happen to everyone you know!'

His cheerful words were greeted with a great deal of laughter, and the poignant moment of that recent parting was instantly forgotten, as they all rushed back across the road and down the drive, towards the marquee, where they knew plenty of food and drink was still available, with dancing in the hall to follow later.

Tim quickly caught up with the very desirable Marcia, and reached for her hand as they ran along side by side.

Now Marcia, because of her profession, had become very worldly wise, and extremely knowledgeable of the idiosyncrasies and peculiar ways of men, consequently she knew exactly how to treat Master Tim Carter, and his excessively large ego!

Of course, bearing in mind the disgusting scene she had witnessed, when last she saw him some three weeks ago, Tim wouldn't have been too surprised if Marcia had snatched her hand away, and told him where to go! But Tim, being Tim, could just not believe that any woman, young or old, could resist his advances for long, and that eventually, if he used the correct bait, he would be able to reel her in, and enjoy this very beautiful succulent dish at his leisure.

'Hello darling.' He panted, as he drew level with the girl who was uppermost in his thoughts. Amazingly, she reciprocated, and was now gripping his hand as they ran along side by side.

'Sorry I couldn't spend any time with you earlier, but of course as you know I was fully occupied being best man to Paul. However, you will be pleased to know, I am all your's for the rest of this glorious day.' Then as an apparent afterthought. 'For the rest of the night too, if you wish, and I can promise it will be just as glorious, if not more so!'

Even as she turned her head and smiled, Marcia shuddered. Evidently she hadn't met them all yet! She had a right one here she thought, as she ran along. The effrontery, the brazen cheek, and the size of this man's ego, must be beyond compare, and Marcia decided she was really going to enjoy herself with Tim Carter, and it would be her who would end this liaison, and not him, as she was correct in assuming, had always been the case in the past!

They made a very attractive couple as they walked in the marquee together, Marcia with her arm through his, and her father was the first to see them.

'Hello you two,' he greeted them, obviously pleased his daughter was in the company of the handsome Tim, and still painfully unaware of the young man's true character.

'Lovely wedding, are you two enjoying yourselves? You certainly should be Marcia, in the company of such a fine looking attentive escort.'

Before his daughter could reply, Tim butted in. 'Thank you Charles, I'm very pleased you said that, though of course it really wasn't necessary. You see, Marcia

50

already knows what kind of an escort she has, don't you darling?'

Marcia even amazed herself by embracing her father and Tim, with one of her most attractive smiles. 'Yes daddy, I'm enjoying myself immensely thank you, and yes dearest Tim, I am very well aware of the kind of escort I have.'

The handsome Tim was far too full of himself, to detect a barb, or the slightest hint of sarcasm in the soft dulcet tones of his beautiful companion. Even if he had, he would never have believed it possible!

At that moment, one of the foremen off the estate, whom Charles had appointed as M.C. for the rest of the festivities called everyone to order, and informed them that dancing was about to commence at Mount Pleasant, in the huge hall.

Almost immediately, an exodus from the marquee began, as the guests began to drift towards the sound of dance music, emanating from the house. A stage had been erected at the far end of the hall, and a five piece band was in full swing, as Marcia and Tim joined the many couples already enjoying the first dance.

The next dance was a waltz, and unknowingly, the haunting music caused Marcia to become lulled into an exaggerated sense of euphoria, as she swayed around the hall in the arms of her partner, for there was no doubt Tim Carter certainly knew how to dance, and she mentally had to shake herself back to reality, when the music stopped.

Tim didn't release her immediately, but held her at arm's length, and gazed adoringly into her beautiful eyes. 'That was wonderful Marcia. You really are a marvellous dancer, we made a perfect couple you know, everyone was watching us!'

She looked up at him, her cheeks flushed, her full red lips parted invitingly, and Tim Carter, never being one to forego an opportunity such as this, crushed her to him, and kissed her passionately, in front of a host of her friends still on the dance floor!

Amazingly, Marcia reciprocated, passion with passion, kiss for kiss, until suddenly, several members of the bemused crowd who were watching, started clapping and cheering, and a few who were slightly the worse for drink, began shouting advice, which unfortunately, cannot possibly be repeated!

The resultant mayhem, seemed to bring Marcia to her senses, and looking round at all the grinning faces, she suddenly seemed to assume an air of injured innocence, almost nonchalance, as she removed her arms from around the neck of her suitor, and led him to the table where a large assortment of drinks were assembled.

'What would you like to drink darling?' she asked, in a voice loud enough for everyone to hear.

'Just a glass of that wonderful looking punch, thank you my dear,' replied Tim, naturally accepting all this adulation as his right.

During the last of three more dances, interspersed with three more glasses of punch, Tim decided it was time to turn on the irresistible Carter charm, and gradually, yet almost imperceptibly, he steered Marcia towards a door at the far end of the hall. Turning his back to the door, he opened it and pretended to fall through, dragging his unsuspecting partner with him.

Quickly standing upright, he closed the door, then guided Marcia towards the first door he could see in front of them. Opening it, he thrust her inside, to discover they were in the library, he then closed and locked the door, whilst still holding her with one hand.

The drink was now beginning to take effect, and Tim, not intending to waste any time, roughly crushed Marcia to him, kissed her, and then began to tear at her clothes!

Marcia, having no intention of being raped, and knowing she could never match his strength, realising she may have taken on more than she had bargained for, quickly assessed the situation, and decided how to treat this lustful drunken braggart, with his overbearing rampant ego.

Melting into his bear like embrace. 'Please darling, there is no need to be so rough,' she purred seductively. 'Just slow down a little, I'm sure we shall both enjoy it so much more.'

He stared down at her unbelievingly, then after a few seconds, found his voice. 'Oh! Marcia,' he drooled, with a slight slur, because of the drink. 'I knew you would never be able to resist me, the moment we were alone.' Then holding her close, he tried to kiss her again.

Marcia, because of her youth, and her profession, was quite strong, and now calling upon all her strength, she suddenly, and very savagely, brought up her knee, right into the groin of her salacious, licentious companion! The sudden expression of astonishment, then absolute agony, upon the countenance of Tim Carter, as he gave a low scream, then clutching his nether regions with both hands, collapsed in an untidy heap at her feet, came as no surprise to Marcia, because of the knowledge of the male anatomy, she had gained through her years of training as a nurse.

Giving one last contemptuous glance at the prostrate figure lying on the library floor, Marcia allowed herself a slow smile. 'No, somehow I don't think you will be bothering me again, Mr.Romeo Carter!' she said softly, as she left the room, closing the door behind her.

As she stepped into the hall, Marcia almost collided with Rose. 'Hello darling,' said Rose. 'I was just coming to look for you. Where is that lovely young man you were dancing with earlier? I thought I saw you leave the dance floor together.'

Marcia hesitated for a second, then quickly decided what to do. 'He is lying on the library floor mummy,' she replied calmly. 'I'm afraid Tim Carter isn't quite the man daddy seems to think he is. For some inexplicable reason, he doesn't appear to be able to control his libido!'

'Good Heavens Marcia. What a thing to say. Where are you going to now?'

Her daughter embraced Rose with a loving sweet smile. 'I'm just going to look for Sam and Bill, then send them in to remove the body.' Marcia was on the point of turning away. 'Please don't mention any of this to daddy. I would hate Tim to lose his job, just because he can't keep his sexual urges in check!' she added with a smile.

After the hall door closed, Rose stood in the corridor staring at the blank space where her beautiful daughter had been, and she wondered. Wherever would she find another young woman, who could have treated this whole disgusting episode, with such charming indifference, even not wanting her father to know about it, in case he sacked Tim Carter!

With a shrug, she turned and walked into the library. The scene that met her eyes, was nearly as her daughter had described, though not quite, for Tim Carter was bent double, and curled up in almost the foetus position, but with both hands clutching his groin. He looked up as the door closed, yet through the pain he was suffering, and the haze still clouding his vision, he could only make out the figure of a woman. *'Now Marcia, you bloody bitch! What the hell have you come back for? Just to gloat, or to have another kick at me? My God! If I could stand, I would rape you now, then bloody strangle you with my bare hands!'*

A shocked Rose momentarily froze, then the miller's daughter quickly asserted herself. 'I don't think that would be a very good idea Mr. Carter,' she said softly. 'In fact, I think it would be a much better idea, if you were to stand up, and get out of this house, as fast as you can!'

The sound of Rose's quiet voice, had a spectacular effect upon the seemingly mortally wounded, sexually inclined rooster. 'Oh! Mrs. Cartwright. Please forgive me. I had no idea it was you standing there, I thought it was the maid, the one who kicked me. I'm terribly sorry,' he finished lamely.

'I don't seem to remember having a maid named Marcia, Mr. Carter!'

At that moment, the door flew open, as Bill and Sam burst in, with Marcia in close attendance. They were two labourers from the quarry, both big strapping lads, who loved nothing better than a fight, yet would do anything for Miss Marcia, and always treated her with the utmost respect. She hadn't dared tell them what the randy Tim had been up to, otherwise they would quite probably have killed him!

Neither of them spoke, as they each gripped an arm of the hapless, unsuspecting Tim, and lifted him clear of the floor, before carrying him out of the door, though a few choice epithets did emanate from the struggling Casanova, as they proceeded along the corridor, before unceremoniously ejecting him through the back door, and out onto the cobbled courtyard!

Meanwhile, Marcia returned to the hall, and rejoined the dancers, to have a thoroughly enjoyable time for the rest of the evening, discovering, somewhat to her surprise, considering the way she had allowed Tim Carter to monopolise her earlier, that she had no shortage of partners, and was in great demand, right up to and including the last waltz.

4

Charles had given Tom and Milly, the use of the Cartwright holiday home at Scarborough for their honeymoon, the one overlooking the Spa, which Thomas had bought whilst on holiday during the last century, and which had been used by members of the Cartwright family, for their annual holiday, every summer since that first time, when he had stayed in Scarborough with his beautiful Maria.

They had enjoyed a wonderful week, and just kept asking each other. Why on earth hadn't they married years ago? However, the happy couple had been home a week, when Paul and his lovely Emma eventually arrived, for they had booked two weeks in France.

Milly was outside tending the cottage garden, and she looked up as she heard the Rolls arrive on the gravelled drive, and pull up at the front entrance to Mount Pleasant. Flinging her fork and gardening gloves to the ground, she ran across the intervening lawns, and reached the car, just as Eric Teesdale opened the door for Emma to step out.

'Hello my darling,' she cried, enfolding the lovely girl in her arms. 'Did you have a wonderful time in France?' But before Emma replied, Milly knew there was something drastically wrong, for her beautiful eyes were red rimmed, and that light which had always shone forth, simply through the sheer joy of living, had somehow become extinguished during those two short weeks!

'Yes thank you,' Emma replied, in a lacklustre voice, then she added in no more than a whisper. 'I'll slip across, and see you later,' before moving away to join her husband, as they climbed the steps together, and disappeared inside, leaving Milly wondering and alone, outside on the drive.

Slowly she turned and retraced her steps back to her cottage, and in deep thought with her head down, almost colliding with Tom. 'I say Milly, you should really look where you're going,' he greeted her facetiously. 'I hope you were thinking of me just then, you were obviously thinking very deeply about something or someone.'

'Emma!' she replied laconically, as she tried, unsuccessfully to raise a smile at her husband's banter. 'I have just met her, and there's definitely something not right Tom.'

As she knew he would, Tom immediately leapt to the defence of his beloved daughter, for she could never do anything wrong in his eyes. 'Emma!' he ejaculated. 'Nonsense Milly, you must be mistaken. What can possibly be wrong? She has just returned from her honeymoon, after being married to Paul Cartwright, the most eligible bachelor in the county, and a perfect gentleman to boot. Why, there are scores of young women who would willingly give their eye teeth, to be in my Emma's shoes, so what on earth do you mean?'

Milly hesitated, she didn't want to spoil things between her and Tom, yet she had this gut feeling, that something was terribly wrong with the life of her beloved Emma, and she would never rest, until she had put it right, or at least discovered what the problem was, even if it placed her own marriage in jeopardy! Therefore, she turned away, and deigned not to reply.

However, Emma didn't slip across to visit her father and her stepmother that evening, so before church the following morning, Tom and Milly walked over to the house, to try and find out what was wrong. A maid answered to Tom's pull upon the bell, and invited them in, taking them to a small room just off the hall, where she suggested they take a seat, and she would inform Mrs. Cartwright they were here.

A few moments later, Rose entered, and bade them sit down again, for they had both jumped up, immediately she came in the room. 'Good morning Milly, morning Tom,' she greeted them lightly. 'How are you both, this bright and happy morn?'

Slightly taken aback, by this cavalier attitude which Rose displayed, Tom hesitated, and Milly, seeing his hesitation, stepped in to fill the breach. 'Very well thank you, but we are worried about Emma. When I met her on the drive yesterday, she didn't seem to be her normal happy-go-lucky self, and she whispered in my ear, that she would slip across and see us later. Well, she never came, so we have called this morning to see her, and to see if she enjoyed her honeymoon.'

Rose smiled. 'Well I'm terribly sorry to disappoint you both, but she is still in bed, she seems to have caught a late summer cold. Probably too much sun in France, whilst on holiday.' She stood up, obviously wanting to bring this interview to an end. 'However, I will tell her you asked after her, and make sure she comes to see you as soon as possible. Thank you both for calling,' she added, as she ushered them from the room.

'Just a minute Rose,' said Tom quietly. 'Are we all going to church this morning as usual, and then coming back here for the Sunday Roast?'

Rose smiled disarmingly. 'Yes Tom, of

course we are. Whatever reason do you have for thinking otherwise? Apart from anything else, this is a very important Sunday. We have to celebrate the homecoming of a rather special couple, our honeymooners, Paul and Emma!'

Before Tom could think of a suitable reply, Rose had closed the massive door, and left he and Milly on the top step, gazing at each other, and realising that neither of them had gleaned a single scrap of information about the welfare of Tom's lovely daughter, and knew no more, than when they had left their cottage twenty minutes earlier.

However, Emma didn't put in an appearance, to go with the rest of the family to church that Sunday morning, and consequently, Milly's mind was never on the service, as she imagined all kinds of dire happenings to her beautiful Emma, since being married to that Paul!

When they all eventually arrived back at Mount Pleasant, and were duly ushered into the dining room, only five places were set at the table, and Milly looked enquiringly at Paul. 'Where is Emma? Isn't she coming down for Sunday dinner?'

Paul averted his eyes before the frank gaze of this woman, who had known his wife since she was a child, and he wondered if she knew what he knew! 'No Milly, I'm sorry, but I don't think she is well enough yet.'

There was no explanation, and Paul's evasive remark and secretive attitude, proved too much for Tom. Turning abruptly, he confronted the unhappy looking, so recently married Paul. 'So, you don't think she is well enough to come downstairs for her Sunday dinner, or to greet her father and her new stepmother?'

'Well, I'm sorry, but I don't believe you.' Then turning to the door. 'If she isn't well enough to come down and meet us, then we will go up and see her. Which room is she in?'

★ ★ ★

Paul immediately positioned himself in front of the doorway. 'No, I'm sorry, I don't think you should do that!'

The set of Tom's jaw hardened, as he unceremoniously thrust the irate young man aside. 'No, and I don't think you should try and stop me! Come along Milly, we shall have to find her bedroom on our own.'

Realising he would be no match for the tall ex-grenadier, Paul responded by pushing past him and Milly, and leading the way upstairs to Emma's room. Quietly opening the door, the three of them filed in, and not knowing what to expect, Milly and Tom were surprised to see a very healthy looking, fully clothed Emma, rush across the room with open arms to meet them both.

'Oh! Daddy, Milly, I'm so pleased you have come', she greeted them, tears welling up in her beautiful eyes. 'I'm terribly unhappy, I really don't know what to do.' Then, for the first time, Emma became aware of her husband's presence. 'It's all his fault, he doesn't seem to care about me anymore,' she wailed, the tears now flowing freely down her satin smooth, youthful looking cheeks.

'That's all right darling,' said her father sympathetically, as he placed a protective arm around her heaving shoulders. 'We will take you home now and sort this mess out, I don't suppose it's more than a storm in a teacup anyway.'

'Oh! but it is daddy! Ask Paul, he will tell you.'

Tom turned to the young man, but he was suddenly extremely reticent, and refused to throw any light upon this furore. He did however, make one remark. 'I don't think it's a very good idea of your's Tom, to take my wife from the marital home to your cottage, even if she is your daughter!'

Milly could see her husband of only a couple of weeks, was about to erupt, and placed a restraining hand upon his arm. 'Don't worry Paul,' she said quietly, calming what she knew to be an imminent explosive situation, and showing a side to her personality, and a latent talent, of which both she and her husband, had hitherto, been totally unaware. 'We are only taking her home to chat, of course she will return here, if and when she wishes. Please remember we haven't seen her for more than two weeks, and naturally have much to talk about. Come along my dear,' said her new stepmother nonchalantly, as she took Emma by the hand, and calmly led her past a bemused looking Paul.

A very proud, though rather subdued Tom Laceby, followed the pair down that beautiful curved staircase, and were accosted by Charles and Rose, as they reached the hall. However, when they saw the expression on Tom's face, and those of his daughter's and Milly's, no-one spoke, as they stepped aside, and allowed the trio to pass.

The three maintained a sombre silence, until they reached the cottage, and had closed the door behind them. Then, when Milly and Emma were seated, Tom addressed his daughter, and though his voice was quiet, there lurked a distinct undertone of irritation behind it, and in his manner. 'Right, my girl.

Now what the hell is all this about?'

Emma knew perfectly well what Paul's problem was, but dare not, under any circumstance or duress, reveal to her father the true nature of it, for she was well aware, he would disown her immediately! So, being the daughter, not only of Tom, but also of the late ravishing, promiscuous Charlotte, she decided to prevaricate!

'I'm sorry daddy, but I don't really know. I do know that when we were first married, Paul couldn't keep his hands off me. Then after we spent our first night together, in a gorgeous honeymoon suite, the following morning he was completely different, very cold and distant, and has never so much as even attempted to kiss me since, in fact he has treated me as one would treat a leper!'

Tom could make no sense of this explanation, and as he had to go and attend to an important matter on the estate, he left his wife and daughter to thrash the matter out between themselves.

When they were alone, Milly placed her arm around the unhappy Emma's shoulders, and drew her close. 'Now tell me all about it darling. What really is the problem with this lovely new husband of your's?'

★ ★ ★

Emma lay her head upon the older woman's shoulder. 'He doesn't love me anymore!', she muttered brokenly. Milly removed her arm, and pushed her companion away from her side. 'Now sit up straight Emma, and look me in the eye!' she said forcefully, gazing at her intently. 'Tell me this young lady. Do you love Paul?'

Emma looked away as she hesitated, then bringing her eyes back to face those of her interrogator, with the tears pricking once more behind her eyelids. 'I-I, don't think so,' she stammered. 'At least not like I did before the wedding. I don't think I shall ever be able to, particularly after the way he treated me, and the names he called me!' she finished with a sob in her throat.

Milly stiffened. 'Names? What names did he call you my precious?'

Again Emma turned her head away. '*After we had made love, he said I was definitely not a virgin before we were married! And that I had performed like a professional prostitute! You know Milly, better than most, how I have inherited this vicious streak when I'm riled from mummy, apart from a few other things, so I tore into him, and asked in no uncertain terms how the hell he came to know so much about prostitutes?*'

A bemused Milly, gazed upon her youthful

companion open mouthed. 'Emma, what a thing to say. What on earth was his reply to that?'

Emma was feeling much better now she had partially unburdened herself of the trauma, which had bothered her since that first horrible morning of the honeymoon, and she actually gave a wan little smile, as she answered Milly's question. '*He said he knew, because he had, on more than one occasion, visited a certain house of ill repute in the city, and that I could teach a few things to the girls who worked there!* Well, upon that remark, I went for him, and hit him with everything I could lay my hands on. The upshot was, he gathered up his things, and ran out of the room, apparently booking another room, somewhere else in the hotel!'

Milly sat in silent thought for a few moments, and at length a rather impatient Emma asked. 'Well Milly, what do you have to say to all this, can you help me?'

Milly lifted her head. 'I don't know darling. Where did you sleep last night? In the same bed I hope.'

Again Emma smiled, though still rather wistfully. 'Yes, we slept in the same bed, though as far apart as possible, and we never touched all night.'

Milly jumped up. 'Alright, now come along

young lady, you and I are going visiting.'

However, Emma didn't move, she just sat there, apparently suffering from another bout of lethargy, and now appearing more despondent and morose than ever.

Her lifelong friend and companion shook her, then spoke quietly. 'There's something else, isn't there darling? Something you haven't told me. What is it?'

As Milly looked at her, she almost cried out at the hurt and pathos, reflected in the lacklustre eyes of her beautiful companion. 'What's troubling you Emma? Please tell me,' she murmured softly.

Suddenly, Emma dropped to her knees, and fell sobbing in the lap of this woman, who had known her since she was a child. 'Oh! Milly, Milly,' she sobbed. 'Please help me. I shall never be able to give Paul a child, even if we do ever manage to get together again. You see, while I was away I made a terrible mistake, and became pregnant. Well obviously, I couldn't possibly have a baby, whilst studying at a college for young ladies, so I took the only way out I knew.'

A speechless, awestruck Milly, sat frozen to the sofa, while aimlessly stroking the beautiful hair, of this apparent stranger, with her head still buried in her lap, and she suddenly realised how little she knew of this young woman, whom she had raised, almost single handed, since the early demise of her mother.

At last, she found her voice. *'Do you mean, you had an abortion?'* she asked in a strained whisper, as though the very words, would bring the devil himself, crashing through the roof!

Emma lifted her tear stained face. 'Yes Milly, that is exactly what I mean, but I'm afraid that's not all.'

'Not all? Good Lord, what else can there be?'

The head bowed again, as a fresh wave of sobbing caused her slim shoulders to shake spasmodically, then with a great effort, Emma seemed to regain a modicum of her normal composure, and still with her head buried in her companion's lap, she mumbled almost incoherently. *'Something went wrong during the abortion, and I shall never be able to conceive, not ever!'*

For some considerable time, silence reigned in that lovely sun lit room, as Milly continued to cradle the head of this beautiful young woman, and her heart went out to her as she recognized her desperate cry for help, knowing there was nothing she could do, while at the same time, again realising how very little she knew of the real Emma!

At last Milly broke this all pervading

silence. 'Well to say you have surprised me with all these revelations, would be an understatement my dear. To be quite honest you have positively shocked me. However, there is no point in crying over spilt milk, as they say, so stand up and dry your eyes my darling, and let's see what you and I can salvage from this unholy mess.'

Emma complied, and Milly passed her a handkerchief, for which she thanked her with a grateful smile. 'Oh! Milly, I feel so terrible burdening you with my appalling problems. I am sure they would never have arisen, if I hadn't inherited this damn sexual addiction thing from mummy!' she added, rather petulantly.

Though Milly's tone was firm, she couldn't help a slight smile just hovering around the corners of her attractive mouth. 'Now steady on Emma. You can't go around blaming Charlotte for your indiscretions, you really must try to curb your sexual appetite, and learn to say no to these predatory males, otherwise when the word spreads, as it surely will, and it becomes generally known how easy you are, they will never leave you alone! Now don't worry yourself unduly, about not being able to have a baby, I mean if Paul refuses to have anything more to do with you, then there is no problem. Anyway, lots of women go through life without having a child, I've never had one, and I don't think I'm any the worse for it. Apart from all that, there is no reason whatsoever, why Paul should ever know anything about your abortion. I don't think you will tell him, and I know for a fact, that I shall certainly never breathe a word to anyone, so therefore my dear, this shall be our secret, just your's and mine!'

They were both standing now, and the troubled Emma flung her arms around her lifelong friend and mentor. 'Oh! Darling Milly, I knew you would understand, I feel so much better now you know everything.'

'What made you so sure I would understand?' Milly asked quietly.

For the first time since entering the cottage, Emma gave a slight chuckle, then replied in a matter of fact voice. 'Because, my dear sweet Milly, you knew mummy, and you also know, that I am so very much like her! Does that answer your question?'

Milly gave no reply as she gazed upon this vision of beauty, for suddenly she became aware of a renewed tide of love, sweeping over her, as she saw once again her beloved Charlotte, in the person of this beautiful daughter of her late mistress, and knew that day, a bond had been forged between them, a bond which only death could break!

After a moment's silence, Emma spoke again. 'I say Milly, did you mention earlier, something about going visiting?'

Milly snapped out of her reverie. 'Why yes dear, with all your revelations, I'm afraid I had forgotten all about it. Personally Emma, I think we should go and tell your Aunt Rose a little of what has transpired this afternoon.'

Emma blanched. 'Oh No! Milly, I couldn't possibly. I'm sorry, but I dare not say a word to anyone else. I only told you, because I had to tell someone, and I trust you implicitly. No, Paul and I shall just have to muddle through on our own, as best we can, and if things become utterly unbearable, then I shall simply pack my belongings, and move back in here with daddy and you!'

At that moment, they heard the garden gate as Tom arrived home, and the conversation ceased.

5

The Gables Private School September 1938

Since the opening of The Gables Private
School, just after The Great War, the two war
widows, Joan and Enid Cartwright, had
continued to attract the sons and daughters
of wealthy parents, and now the school had
an attendance of some fifty pupils.

Of the three daughters Joan and her late
husband had brought into the world, two had
married successful businessmen in the city,
whilst the third and youngest, had opted for
the nursing profession, and was living in the
nurse's accommodation, at the same hospital
as her cousin, Marcia.

Of Enid's two children, her son had
followed in his mother's footsteps, and after
Cambridge, was teaching at a public school,
somewhere south of London.

His sister Anne, had also inherited a
fondness for teaching, but after university, she
had decided to come home, to join her
mother and her Aunt Joan, and teach at The
Gables.

Owing to the continued improvement in

travel and communications, parents of a few of the students, had suggested to Enid and Joan, that it might be a good idea to employ a French teacher, to enable their offspring to converse with the natives, when on holiday abroad.

This idea was subsequently mooted at the next meeting of the School Governors, which included Charles and Rose. The consequence of this, was an advertisement being placed in the relevant journal, for a French teacher, preferably young and female. The article also stated, that living accommodation would be provided.

During the following weeks, two young female hopefuls, came knocking on the door of The Gables, and applied for the post of French teacher. However, both were unsuccessful, and the two Principals were on the point of scrapping the whole scheme, when on the last Saturday of the third week after placing the advertisement, the doorbell rang.

Joan happened to be in the hall, and went to open the door. An elfin faced, beautiful young woman was standing there.

'Pardon me. Please is this The Gables Private School'? she asked, in impeccable English, yet with a distinctive French accent.

Joan greeted the stranger with a welcoming smile, as she thought. 'I think this may be the one' 'Yes my dear this is The Gables, why do you ask?'

'Because, if this is The Gables School, I have come in reply to your advertisement in this magazine,' she withdrew the paper from her bag as she spoke.

Joan opened the door a little wider. 'Do please come in my dear,' she said, bestowing another smile upon this lovely girl, as she added. 'And please follow me.'

At that moment, another door opened further down the hall, and Enid stepped out, hesitating when she saw Joan coming towards her, accompanied by a beautiful, very French looking, petite young woman.

As they approached, Enid held up her hand. 'Don't bother to tell me Joan, this young lady hopes to become our new French teacher.'

They looked at her in surprise. 'However did you know that?' asked a bemused Joan.

Enid laughed aloud. 'Because my dear, your companion appears so deliciously French, also the magazine she is holding, just happens to be open at the page of our advertisement for a French teacher.'

The young stranger and Joan looked down at the open magazine, and immediately joined in the laughter. 'Yes, of course you're quite right dear,' said Joan, endeavouring to suppress another bout of merriment. 'I think, this time we may have found the right one, come into the office, both of you.'

She led the way with Joan and the young lady following in her wake, into a small room just off the hall, which served as a comfortable, and apparently a very efficient looking office. Joan seated herself, and motioned the others to do likewise, then after pressing a button fitted on her desk to summon the maid, and ordering tea and biscuits, she proceeded to interview this young beautiful applicant, for the new post of French mistress.

'What is your name my dear?' she asked, and though the voice was kindly, the prospective teacher detected a note of authority in her tone.

'My name is Margurite. Please, how do I call you?' she asked quietly, with just that slight hint of a French accent, which is so endearing to the English.

Her interrogator smiled. 'Sorry Margurite, I should have made the introductions earlier. You may call us by our Christian names. I am Joan, and this is Enid, we are partners and co-owners of The Gables, which we opened as a private school just after the war. We then had about a dozen pupils, and we now have approximately fifty, twenty of whom are boarders.'

'Excuse please. What are borders?'

Again Joan smiled. 'Boarders my dear, are pupils who live in, stay here at The Gables, and only return home at the end of term.'

'Of course, how silly of me. Please, shall I become a boarder? Will I live in?'

Joan and Enid wanted to laugh, but they couldn't, because of the sweet innocent way Margurite asked her questions, and as the interview continued, they both became completely captivated by this very modern, very chic, gorgeous looking French girl, and finally they had no hesitation in offering her the very important position of the new French mistress at The Gables.

Margurite accepted with relish and great excitement, and Joan poured each of them a glass of sherry to celebrate this rather auspicious occasion. When the atmosphere had calmed down a little, and after emptying her glass, Margurite spoke. 'Please, may I go to bring in my case.'

Her new employers appeared surprised. 'Your case? Where is it?' asked Joan.

'Outside, I left it there, because I thought, I might not be staying.'

Again Joan pressed the button upon her desk, and when the maid appeared she instructed her to tell one of the senior boys, to fetch the suitcase and leave it in the hall.

A few moments later they heard sounds outside the office door, and Joan immediately went to investigate. 'Come along Margurite,' she called over her shoulder. 'We will take you to your room.'

They were in the hall now, and a young man was just walking away from a rather large leather suitcase. 'Ah! Chivers,' called Joan. 'Please be a good chap, and carry that case upstairs for Mademoiselle. Yes Chivers, I know she is lovely, but there's no need to gawp boy. Good Heavens! Where are your manners? However, this is Margurite, our new French teacher.

Do you approve?'

The youth smiled and nodded towards this vision of beauty, apparently dumbstruck, he had never in all his life seen any school-teacher, who looked anything like this beauty, and he just couldn't wait to return to his friends, and tell them his wonderful news!

A sudden thought struck him, and he turned to Joan. 'You do have my name down for French lessons, don't you Miss?'

Joan smiled, along with her companions. 'Yes Chivers, your name is on the list, just as you and your parents requested. Now come along, and let's have this case taken to Miss Margurite's room.'

Chivers responded with alacrity, and

struggled to make the heavy case appear of no consequence, as though it was stuffed full of feathers, endeavouring to give a good impression of himself, for the benefit of the delectable Margurite.

The maid was leading the small procession, and she halted at the third door along the landing, opened it, then stepped aside, to allow Margurite to enter.

Her room was at the front of the house, overlooking sweeping lawns, which sloped down towards the main road, and as she entered this sun filled room, the new teacher cried out with sheer pleasure. 'Oh! what a beautiful room. Please, are you sure this is the correct one?' Then without waiting for a reply, she crossed to the large bow window. 'And just look at this splendid view. Through the trees I can see the sun sparkling on some water. Is that a river?'

Joan had to smile at Margurite's unaffected exuberance. 'Yes dear, that is the River Humber, Enid and I will take you down to see it sometime soon, then next summer on a fine day, we will go and have a picnic on the river bank. Would you like that Margurite?'

Her beautiful blue eyes literally sparkled. 'Oo! Yes please. I love going to picnic. What a lovely inviting big bed,' she remarked, as she turned from the window. 'You will never be able to wake me in the mornings,' she added with a chuckle.

Her companions laughed with her, and after Chivers had deposited her case upon a chair, they left her with the maid to help her unpack, and hang her clothes in the wardrobe, and then to show her where the bathroom was.

On the way downstairs, Joan turned to her friend and partner. 'Well Enid, I do believe we have found a real treasure this time. I sincerely hope she likes us, and decides to stay.'

Enid looked in some surprise at her companion. 'Of course she will stay, whatever can give you cause to think otherwise?'

Joan hesitated, but only momentarily. 'I don't know,' she said slowly. 'You see, she is so beautiful, and has such a stunning figure, and a wonderful personality, when word gets around, as it undoubtedly will, we shall have every rampant, predatory bachelor from miles around, knocking on our front door!'

However, as the weeks slipped by, only part of Joan's prophesy was proved to be correct, for many a hopeful young Lothario did call, as she had predicted, but the one who succeeded in stealing the heart of this lovely young French miss, just happened to be the only one among them, who was not a bachelor!

6

Late Spring 1939

Once again the drums of war were beating out across Europe, and Hitler was beginning to show himself as a real danger to the civilised world.

While 'Anderson' air raid shelters had now been distributed throughout the length and breadth of Britain, and on the twenty seventh of April, the British Government had introduced conscription for all young men for military service, on May the twenty second, Italy and Germany forged a Fascist Alliance, named the 'Pact of Steel', a military and political alliance, committing them to support each other with total military forces, in time of war!

For since Chamberlain had returned home from Munich, waving that now infamous piece of paper, 'Declaring Peace In Our Time,' Hitler had invaded Czechoslovakia, and was now making threatening overtures to Poland.

This was regarded so seriously by His Majesty's Government, that Chamberlain made an historic statement in The House, being cheered from all sides. 'That Britain and France, are now pledged to defend Poland against an attack!'

These apocalyptic war mongering rumours seesawing to and fro across the Continent of Europe, seemed light years away from a lovely young woman enjoying a leisurely stroll down a quiet English country lane, within the boundary of her father's estate, on this beautiful late spring evening.

Marcia began to sing softly to herself as she walked along. Moments later, her singing and her thoughts were rudely interrupted by a man leaping out in front of her, through an open gateway to a field, from behind the hedge, where he had been hiding.

Marcia paled as she recognized him. 'What do you want Tim Carter?' she demanded angrily.

Tim emitted a harsh triumphant laugh. 'I think you already know the answer to that question,' he replied.

Marcia trembled at the inference, as she recalled their last meeting, and as she moved to pass him, he grabbed her by the wrist, and dragged her into the field. Flinging her down upon the grass, he began to tear at her clothes.

'I'll teach you to kick me in the groin, you

stuck up little bitch. Nobody does that to Tim Carter and gets away with it. You led me on that night, Miss Bloody Marcia. Well now you're going to pay for it!'

Finally, after a struggle, he had removed her dress and pants, and as he stood up to unbuckle his belt and allow his trousers to fall to the ground, the terrified Marcia, knowing she could never match his strength, suddenly thought of something a colleague had once told her. 'If you are ever attacked my girl, always remember a young woman can run far faster with her pants in her hand, than a bloke can with his trousers round his ankles!'

With this desperate thought in mind, she grabbed her clothes, leapt up off the grass, and bolted through the open gateway, tearing off up the road, the way she had come, leaving her enraged salacious attacker screaming obscenities after her.

For a while her friend's advice proved to be correct, for as Tim struggled to pull up his trousers and fasten his belt, Marcia had managed to leave him a good hundred yards behind. However, with his much longer stride, he steadily began to overhaul the now freely perspiring Marcia, and he was within an arm's length of reaching out to grab her by the hair, when, on hearing a thunderous noise immediately behind, he turned his head, just in time to see a body with flailing arms and legs, leap off a sweating horse, and hurtle straight towards him!

As a winded Tim Carter hit the hard road, an angry ferocious Eric Teesdale, sat astride the inert body, and with apparent murderous intent, smashed both his knotted fists into what had once been the handsome face of this lustful would be rapist, all the time muttering through clenched teeth, *'I'll kill you, you dirty rotten filthy bastard!'*

Meanwhile, as the loose horse flashed past Marcia, and she heard the noise behind her, she suddenly realised that some extraordinary kind of miracle must have taken place, and wonder of wonders, she had been saved!

It was then, as she turned, she saw who her saviour was, and running towards him, she bent low and wrapped her arms around his neck. 'Oh! Eric, Eric, thank you so much. I shall be forever in your debt.' As she held him, and with her eyes brimming with tears, after her remarkable rescue, she realised he was smashing his fists into the now bloodied face of her rampant attacker.

'Stop it now Eric! You will kill him!'

'That would be too good for this animal, after what he was trying to do to you miss,' muttered the head groom, as he reluctantly ceased his pummelling of the now uncon-scious Tim, and eased himself off the inert body. Still on one knee, he looked up startled, then quickly looked away again.

For the very delectable near naked Miss Marcia, was spilling out of her torn and ragged underwear, and manifesting a great sense of decency and gentlemanly conduct, though it has to be admitted, much against his will! Eric whipped off his hacking jacket, and passed it to the trembling, humiliated daughter of his employer. Then keeping his eyes averted, he picked up her pants, and silently handed them to her.

The grateful smile she bestowed upon him, and the look in her beautiful eyes, were all the thanks he needed, and when she was dressed, he caught and mounted his horse, reaching down and helping her up to sit firmly behind him, with her hands in front, clasped tightly around his waist.

Dusk was falling as Eric quietly approached the stables from the rear, gently leading his horse, to make as little noise as possible. Halting at the stable door, he helped Marcia dismount. 'Please wait here miss, while I put him in the stable,' he said in a low voice.

A moment later, he reappeared and led Marcia through a side door, and up a flight of stairs, pausing on a small landing at the top, while he produced a latch key and opened the door to his flat.

Marcia was pleasantly surprised by the size of the place, and also how neat and tidy everything was, considering this was a bachelor's apartment. Meanwhile, Eric had crossed swiftly to the window and drawn the curtains, before switching on a rather attractive standard lamp.

As he turned, Marcia removed his jacket and handed it to him, Eric caught his breath, as he saw the white alabaster of her flawless skin, reflecting the soft glow from the lamp, for of course she was still almost naked.

'If you remove your torn underskirt, I will give you a needle and thread so you can repair it, while I iron your badly creased dress,' he murmured tremulously, fighting for self control, as he realised how beautiful and desirable she was.

★   ★   ★

Quickly looking away as she removed her undergarment, Eric threw a couple of small logs on the dying embers in the grate, and then, thankful for something to do, searched for a needle and thread.

They were standing very close as he passed

them to her, and at that precise moment, they heard the door open, and Emma burst into the room!

'Oh! Eric darling, I thought you were never — !' She stopped dead in her tracks, her mouth still wide open.

'Hello Emma,' said Eric nonchalantly. 'We've had a spot of trouble, Marcia and me, and we are just trying to patch things up a bit.'

Emma closed her mouth like a trap, then immediately opened it again. *'Spot of trouble? Believe me you have no idea what trouble is. Just wait until I tell Uncle Charles what I have found going on in here tonight. You'll be off up the road so bloody fast, they won't be able to see you for dust!'*

Eric was quickly losing his patience. 'Now just you listen to me Emma Laceby. There is absolutely nothing between Miss Marcia and me, she had a slight accident, and rather than tell her parents, I thought it would be a good idea to bring her here, and help her to make herself look more presentable, before taking her home.'

Emma laughed, though her eyes and her mouth were not smiling, and Eric Teesdale shuddered, for that laugh had been very reminiscent of one he had heard just once before, many years ago, and that had come from the late Charlotte, Emma's mother!

'A likely tale. Who the hell do you think is going to believe a load of old clap trap like that?' she asked in a voice heavy with sarcasm.

'Obviously no-one with a mind like a sewer, which is what you apparently have,' came the cold riposte from Marcia.

'Oh! Listen to little miss goody two shoes. And to think, we all thought butter wouldn't melt in her mouth. Still I bet she can't give you the same satisfaction I can Eric!'

Upon that remark, Eric grabbed the ill-mannered, caustic Emma by the scruff of her neck, forcibly marched her to the door, and literally threw her out!

'*You will be sorry for this night's work Eric Teesdale, you dirty two timing bastard!*' she screamed at him, from the other side of the door.

'I'm very sorry about that intrusion Miss Marcia,' said Eric sheepishly, as he produced an iron for her crumpled dress.

Marcia was surprised at the professional way he proceeded to iron out the creases, and thought, what a waste! For there was no doubt, Eric could have made some very lucky girl, a wonderful husband!

Finally the ironing and the repairs to

Marcia's apparel were completed, and when she had finished dressing, she looked down at herself with an undisguised look of approval. 'Thank you very much Eric, you really are a marvel. Apart from saving me earlier, from a fate worse than death,' Marcia hesitated, as she shuddered at the memory. 'At the hands of that horrible over sexed beast, you then bring me back here to your flat, and repair the damage, not only to my clothes, but also to my dignity.'

He appeared embarrassed. 'I was only doing my job miss,' Eric muttered, as he closed the door, and led her downstairs.

Eric walked with her to the front door of Mount Pleasant, and was on the point of turning away, when Marcia gripped his hand, then kissed him, full upon the lips. 'Thank you once again dear Eric,' she whispered, the emotion spilling out through her voice. 'I shall be forever in your debt, I shall never forget how you helped me tonight, and I promise, one day, I shall try and repay you for your kindness!'

Before he could even think of a suitable reply, Marcia had opened the door, and slipped inside.

★   ★   ★

For her main Christmas present that year, Charles had bought his daughter a new car, and on the morning following her miraculous escape from that scurrilous rapist Tim Carter, unfortunately, she was scheduled for an early shift at the hospital.

Because of this, of course Marcia was completely unaware of what transpired at Mount Pleasant, after she left.

On the following Tuesday evening, a very angry and disappointed Rose and Charles, were in the sitting room, impatiently awaiting the return of their daughter, for they knew she had every alternate Wednesday off, and were expecting her at any moment. No words passed between them as they waited, for there had already been far too many, coupled with a great deal of acrimony. So now, all they could do was sit and wait to hear Marcia's version of that terrible night's events.

The evening was cool, and Rose jumped as a log crackled on the fire, sounding almost like the crack of a rifle, as it sliced through the tense atmosphere of this otherwise silent room.

Suddenly they both stiffened at the sound of a car approaching down the gravelled drive. Rose stole a quick, surreptitious glance at her husband, and became more concerned about the impending fate of their daughter, when she saw the determined set of that pugnacious Cartwright jaw.

Time seemed to stand still, as they heard the car door slam, the crunch of gravel underfoot, the front door open, and then close behind her. Her light step as she crossed the hall, and then, she was in the room, looking radiant in a new dress.

Charles, all the tension of the last hours, finally broken, leapt to his feet. *'I don't know how you have the nerve to come here, to call this your home, you dirty little trollop!'* he thundered. *'It nearly killed your mother, when we heard about you and that filthy scheming little bugger, Eric Teesdale!'*

⋆ ⋆ ⋆

Marcia, had stopped transfixed, just inside the room, she stood proud and ramrod straight, her face chalk white, yet her eyes were blazing, first with disbelief, then with righteous anger, as she faced her irate parent.

'So!' The single word was no more than a sibilant hiss, but it should have given her parents ample warning, there was much more to come!

'That lying devious whore Emma, managed to get her story in first, she said she would. But I wasn't worried, you see I

evidently made the ghastly mistake of thinking you would never believe her. Apparently, I was terribly wrong!'

Marcia was the one who was advancing now, as she strode purposefully further into the room, her father retreating before this spate of unprecedented wrath, from the daughter he had worshipped since the day she was born, and even in that electric charged atmosphere, he reflected, he had never seen her looking more beautiful!

'How could either of you, ever believe such an evil story about me? God! You make me sick! I really think the time has come, for you both to learn a few home truths about one of our relatives, also father, a certain favourite member of your staff at the shipyard. What did Emma tell you about that night?'

Charles endeavoured to assert a modicum of authority, over this hitherto unknown ferocious daughter. 'Now just you listen to me my girl, you're not too old for the strap you know!' He tried to sound angry, but he was weakening, for his heart wasn't really in it. Rose had persistently told him, that Emma had been lying all along, however, he pressed doggedly on.

'Emma told us, she heard strange sounds coming from Eric Teesdale's flat above the garage, and went to investigate. She said, she found you and Teesdale in bed together, both of you stripped naked, and that he jumped out of bed, and threw her out!'

Again Charles retreated a step, when he saw the look upon his daughter's face, and the contempt in her eyes. *'And you believed that!'* she shot at him. Suddenly, drawing deeply upon previously unknown reserves, and showing remarkable self control, Marcia became quite calm. 'Just sit down upon the sofa next to mummy, and I'll tell you what really happened,' she said coldly.

Marcia then proceeded to inform her parents of everything that had happened to her, on that fateful evening walk, of how Eric had come along just in time to rescue her from an intended rape, by that sex mad beast Tim Carter, and how kind and decent he had proved to be afterwards. As she finished she turned to Charles. 'In fact, I think you should send for Eric now daddy, to thank him for my rescue, and for the wonderful way he attended to me afterwards.'

Her father turned away, unable to face his daughter, and walking over to the window, he stood there, and stared out with unseeing eyes.

Marcia followed, and stood beside him.

95

'Daddy, I asked you to send for Eric. Why did you walk away?'

Unable to offer her any cogent reply, after the revelations she had just made about Emma and Tim Carter, Charles continued to stare out the window. 'I can't send for Teesdale my dear,' he replied lamely.

'What do you mean, you can't send for him daddy. I'll ring for Sally, and send for him myself.' As she finished speaking, Marcia moved to pull the tassled cord, intending to summon the maid, but her father leapt forward to intercept her.

'*No Marcia!*' he said harshly, as he roughly pushed her away. '*It is no use sending for Teesdale, he won't be there!*'

Marcia appeared hurt and then puzzled. 'Whatever do you mean father?' Still unable or unwilling to accept the terrible truth. 'Of course he will be there.'

Rose, who had remained silent throughout this highly charged, very unpleasant interlude, realised her husband baulked at telling his lovely daughter what had actually happened to Eric, and decided to step in to fill the breach.

'Eric Teesdale won't be there Marcia darling, because he left the following morning, just after you went to the hospital!'

Marcia stood perfectly still, her expression

a mixture of puzzled disbelief, while she allowed that last remark to sink in. Finally, she slowly turned and faced her father. *'Eric did not leave voluntarily did he father? You sacked him, didn't you?'* Her voice was smooth as silk, almost a caress. *'You sacked him, simply on the word of that bitch Emma. You couldn't even wait to hear my version of the events of that night. I don't suppose for a moment, that it ever occurred to any of you, to ask Emma, how she came to have a key to Eric's flat!'*

That last subtle remark struck home like a barb, and Charles wilted before this quiet verbal onslaught, from the beautiful daughter he adored. He almost collapsed in the nearest chair, and keeping his eyes averted, spoke barely above a whisper.

'I'm dreadfully, deeply sorry for what I have done my darling, there is no excuse for the pain I have caused you and Teesdale, or for doubting your integrity in the first place. I should have known you are quite incapable of agreeing to the vile despicable actions, Emma accused you of.'

Suddenly, and without warning, his countenance took on a new expression, as a fresh determined look, replaced the sheepish hang dog appearance he had displayed, since Marcia had pointed out the error of his ways.

Moving over to the fireplace, Charles gave a sharp tug upon the tasseled cord, and almost immediately there was a light knock on the door, then Sally entered the room. 'Ah! Sally, please go and inform Mr.Laceby, I wish to see him now, that will be all.'

★ ★ ★

'What on earth are you going to say to him father? You know how he worships his beloved daughter, she can do no wrong in his eyes,' said a tremulous Marcia, for she knew how difficult and irrational Tom could be, where his precious Emma was concerned, and she had no wish to be instrumental in getting the estate manager the sack.

For the first time since she had entered the room, Charles smiled fondly upon his only daughter. 'Now don't you worry your pretty head about that my dear,' he replied genially. 'From now on, I shall be very careful regarding anything I may say or do, which is remotely connected with you.'

Marcia ran across the room, and flinging her arms around his neck, she kissed him. 'Oh! Daddy, thank you so much for believing in me, really I couldn't bear it, if you didn't trust me.'

At that moment, Sally returned with Tom Laceby.

'I see it didn't take very long Charles, for that young miss to wrap you around her little finger!'

By the way his employer turned on him, Tom knew immediately, he had made a terrible mistake.

'Don't you ever again refer to my daughter in those terms Laceby, otherwise you and I will be parting company!' Charles thundered. 'After what I have heard this night, it is very apparent you should be paying more attention to the kind of life your own daughter leads. Now I want you to go into Hull at first light tomorrow morning, find Eric Teesdale, bring him back here with you, and reinstate him in his old job as head groom!'

The estate manager's countenance reflected a remarkable amalgam of varying expressions, until he finally managed to find his voice, and blurted out. 'Eric Teesdale? Bring him back here? After what he did to your daughter? Are you mad Charles? And what did you mean, pay more attention to my daughter?'

Charles, his fury being spent, was much calmer now. 'I mean Tom, everything Emma told us about that night, was all lies!

A total fabrication from beginning to end. I agree Marcia was in Teesdale's flat. Apparently, he had taken her there, to help her recover, after he had miraculously rescued her, from an attempted rape, by that villainous rascal, young Tim Carter!'

A somewhat subdued Tom Laceby, sat down upon the nearest chair, any fight he may have harboured, completely knocked out of him. 'If what you say is true, then why the devil did Emma manufacture all those lies?' he asked, rather plaintively, Rose thought.

Marcia stepped in. 'Because she was insanely jealous at finding me alone with Eric in his flat. I suspect they had been secret lovers for some time. Please believe me, I'm terribly sorry about all of this Mr.Laceby, but I had to clear my name, and Eric's of course. Just ask your daughter, why she had a key to Eric Teesdale's flat, her answer should help you to arrive at your own conclusion. You see the door to the flat was locked, yet Emma let herself in with her own key!'

The estate manager and his employer's family parted company amicably that night, and that last remark of Marcia's apparently bore fruit.

For Emma Laceby, originally the Lady Emma Brackley, the beautiful, promiscuous daughter, of a beautiful wayward mother, carried her case and a few belongings, out to the car her father was driving, as a tearful Milly waved goodbye, very early the following morning, and everyone thought she would never be seen on the Cartwright estate, ever again!

7

Paul and The New French Mistress

The marriage, between Paul and Emma, which everyone thought had been made in Heaven, was now well and truly over, with not the slightest chance of them ever returning to the matrimonial bed together!

For since that last unsavoury scandal involving Marcia and Eric Teesdale, of which both were completely vindicated, and Emma was proved to be an unmitigated liar, adulteress and much much more, she had been ejected from her father's cottage on the Cartwright estate, and was now living somewhere in Hull.

However, Paul rather surprisingly, quickly got over his estrangement from the beautiful precocious Emma, for upon finding that work wasn't quite sufficient to fill this void in his life, he had recently discovered a new outlet for his many, undoubted talents.

After a chance meeting in Hull one Saturday morning with Joan and Enid, it was suggested, that if he could ever find the time from his busy schedule, it would be very much appreciated if he could go along to The Gables, and give a business lecture occasionally to the older pupils.

For some inexplicable reason, which upon reflection he had never been able to comprehend, and which was totally out of character, Paul had made an unprecedented snap decision, and had immediately agreed to comply. Consequently, today was his third visit in as many weeks, yet utterly unknown to him, this day was to be, as no other had ever been, and would literally, result in being the first day of a new life!

After parking his car near the stables, at the rear of the house, instead of going straight indoors, as was his custom, it was such a beautiful morning, he decided to take a walk through the gardens, for he thought they looked so lovely and fresh in the spring sunshine.

He was walking slowly, totally immersed in his thoughts of the coming lecture, and what he was going to say, when on rounding a corner of the tall hedge, they nearly collided! Paul, in a reflex action, almost before he saw her, instinctively held out his arms to protect himself, and the girl practically walked right into them!

When he realised what he was holding, Paul didn't immediately release her. She was small and petite, almost a head shorter than himself, her dark blue lustrous eyes, were sparkling with vitality and the joy of living. In a word, she was beautiful! At last he seemed to grasp the enormity of the situation, yet owing to the monastic lifestyle he had led, during the recent months, and the glorious fragrance emanating from this lovely girl, coupled with the sheer femininity of her, almost proved too much.

However, Paul's strict upbringing finally won the day, and very reluctantly he gradually eased her warm youthful body away from his own, as he began to apologise most profusely.

'I'm terribly sorry,' he stammered. 'My thoughts were miles away, and I never even saw you until you were in my arms. Do please forgive me.'

She smiled, a wonderfully captivating kind of smile, and in that split second, Paul Cartwright knew he was lost. At least his heart most definitely was!

'There is no need for apologise too much,' she said, laughingly.

Instantly, Paul became more interested in this lovely girl. Her voice was soft, almost like a caress, and apparently she possessed a wonderfully attractive foreign accent. Fortunately, he had taken French at college, and immediately thought she was French.

Suddenly realising they had not even exchanged introductions, Paul thrust out his hand. 'Paul Cartwright at your service, please tell me, what is your name?'

★ ★ ★

Smiling, she placed her dainty hand in his strong masculine one. 'Very pleased to make your acquaintance Paul Cartwright, my name is Margurite.'

Her hand was warm, and Paul experienced a thrill as he shook hands with her, and throwing all caution to the winds, he held on. However, she didn't seem to mind, as she made no effort to release herself from his grip. At length he found his voice. 'Margurite,' his voice was high, he coughed and began again. 'Sorry. Margurite, I think that is a French name, am I correct?'

Still holding his hand, she laughed again, her laugh was infectious, and Paul joined in, reflecting he couldn't remember the last time he had laughed aloud. 'Yes, you are very clever. I hope you guessed that because of my name, and not the accent. I am the new French mistress here at The Gables School,' she added proudly. 'Please tell me, why are you here? Do you work in garden?'

This time it was Paul's turn to smile. 'No my dear, I do not work in garden, as you so beautifully phrase it. The ladies who own this school, are relatives of mine, and since the break up of my marriage last year, they suggested I might wish to give an occasional business lecture to the older pupils, if I could spare the time. So I come once a week, and this is my third week,' he suddenly realised he was rambling on, never in his life before, had he discussed his private affairs with a total stranger! Yet somehow, this girl didn't seem like a stranger, he knew she never would, for he felt he had known her for years!

They began to walk through the garden together, still holding hands. She turned her head, and allowed her lovely eyes to wash over him, at length she spoke. 'So, you are not married?'

His heart leapt, and he tightened his grip upon her hand. Lord! She was sufficiently interested to discover if he was married! He looked straight ahead. 'No, I am not married,' he hesitated. 'Well, yes I am in a way, but we do not live together. You see, my ex wife lives in Hull, and I live about one mile from here.'

As he finished speaking, she reciprocated with a tighter grip upon his hand. 'So,' she spoke slowly. 'Your wife and you, are, how do you say? You are separate?'

Paul laughed, he couldn't help it! Then on a mad sudden impulse, he crushed this lovely girl to him, and kissed her, hard and long! She replied, kiss with passionate kiss, until finally, he had to break this tide of unprecedented emotion, which was beginning to overwhelm him, for it was months since he'd had close personal contact with any member of the fair sex.

She appeared hurt, as he broke this spell which had so suddenly engulfed them, and held her at arm's length. 'Why did you laugh, and then stop kissing me?' she asked, her voice no more than a whisper.

His heart was drumming so hard against his ribs, he was sure she would hear it, and he knew his face was burning, yet he was almost jumping out of his skin with excitement. This lovely girl had returned his kisses!

'Sorry my darling. May I call you my darling?' Whether Margurite agreed or not, Paul didn't wait to find out. 'I laughed because of the delicious way you asked. You are separate? You see my sweet, you should have said. Are you separated? Regarding the second part of your question, I just had to stop kissing you Margurite, otherwise I would probably have dragged you down among these lovely spring flowers, and made glorious love to you!' Paul stopped speaking, amazed at the things he had just said, never in his life, had he ever spoken to any member of the opposite sex in terms like that, and to make such remarks to a complete stranger, really was unforgivable!

Apparently however, his beautiful new friend didn't agree with those sentiments. 'Oh! Darling Paul,' she cried, as she blushed prettily, and embraced him with her lovely dark eyes, which to him, seemed so full of promise! 'I am sure, that would have been so wonderful!' She glanced at the watch upon her wrist. 'Oh! Damn! Look at the time Paul, I have lesson to teach in five minutes.'

Paul smiled wistfully to himself, as he again took her hand, and led her to The Gables rear entrance. 'Yes my dear, so have I, lesson to teach in five minutes.'

★ ★ ★

She turned her head and looked at him, and saw the laughter in his eyes. 'You make fun of my English, yes?' she said. 'What mistake did I say this time?'

He laughed outright. 'No mistake darling Margurite, it is just the wonderful way you have with words, that makes your accent so endearing.'

They stopped just inside the entrance, and for a second time that day, he embraced her pliant wonderful body, as they indulged in what could only be described as a very passionate, lover's kiss.

'When can I see you again?' Paul gasped, as he came up for air.

She held him tight. 'Whenever you wish my darling. I do live here, you know.'

'Very well, if I don't see you later today, I will see you tonight,' as he finished speaking, she gave him one more quick kiss, and expertly slipped out of his arms, before running down the corridor, to her class.

However, Paul did happen to see his new love later that day, but only for a moment, still long enough to tell her to be ready by half-past-six that evening, when he would call and take her out to dinner!

Joan and Enid were quite concerned at the strange behaviour of their recently acquired French school mistress, for immediately after tea that afternoon, of which she had eaten only a morsel, an excited Margurite, acting almost like a teenager, had dashed upstairs to her room. That was nearly two hours ago, and no-one had seen or heard her since.

★ ★ ★

Joan suddenly broke the all pervading silence. 'There's a car coming down the drive,' she said, removing her spectacles, as she closed the book which she had been reading so avidly. Then glancing once more out the window. 'Why I do believe. Yes it is! It's Paul in his new car! Now I wonder what on earth he wants at this hour.'

However, before Enid could even think of a reply, Joan's question was answered with a vengeance, for the door suddenly burst open, and a vision of youth and beauty rushed into the room, fragrantly perfumed, and outrageously feminine in a lovely new evening dress, which neither of her astonished companions had previously seen.

So surprised were they, that before they had time to comment upon her appearance, Paul was in the room, but even he seemed to be struck dumb by this ravishing creature, awaiting his arrival.

Margurite was the first to speak. 'Good evening Paul,' she greeted him calmly. 'I am so pleased to see you.' She turned to her employers. 'I am so sorry, I should have told you Paul is taking me out to dinner this evening. Please say you are happy for me.'

Joan and Enid, though still trying to recover from this sudden unexpected revelation, had to smile, and at last Joan found her voice. 'Yes my dear, of course we are happy for you, aren't we Enid?'

Enid nodded, it seemed to be all she could manage at the moment.

★ ★ ★

Paul, who was gradually recovering from the shock of seeing the real beauty of his new friend for the first time, she appeared so vastly different to the young girl he had met earlier that day in the garden, still couldn't tear his eyes away, at length managed to speak. 'Darling, you look marvellous,' he enthused.' Then addressing the two proprietors of The Gables, whilst still allowing his gaze to feast upon the French mistress. 'I hope you don't mind me taking Margurite out for dinner this evening. I promise to take great care of her, and also to return at a reasonable time.'

'No, of course we don't mind,' replied Joan airily, at the same time, wondering where and when, these two had met.

'What a splendid motorcar,' Margurite exclaimed, as Paul opened the door for her, and she lowered herself gracefully onto the leather seat, revealing a fair amount of her very shapely legs.

When Paul had seen that smart red

M.G.sports car, owned by a certain Dr.Ralph Skinner, he had immediately decided he must have one himself, and had only received it yesterday. Now, as he watched Margurite settle herself into the low seat, he instinctively knew, he would never regret his purchase!

Margurite's hair style was boyishly short, and she loved the wind blowing through her curls, as they sped along in the open car.

Paul finally pulled up in front of a lovely old country inn, with splendid views over the river, and she was enthralled when he led her to a table by the window, which he had previously reserved.

They talked animatedly and incessantly, all through the meal, and of course Paul asked his lovely companion to choose the wine, thinking with her being French, she probably knew far more about the subject than he did. Evidently, she chose a very good one, for the wine seemed to flow just as much as the conversation.

Apparently Margurite loved sailing, and became ecstatic when he told her about the Charlotte Rose, especially when he promised to take her for a sail up the River Humber.

It really was amazing the vast amount of different subjects, these two virtual strangers had in common, and Paul discovered that the lovely Margurite possessed not only a wonderful personality, but also that very fascinating, very rare gift of making him feel as though he was the only other person in the room!

Since meeting her earlier that day, Paul had spent some time doing quite an amount of serious thinking about his future, and knowing he and Emma would never resolve their estrangement, after the appalling way she had behaved, he had decided, that if this evening turned out to be a reasonable success, and providing the lady agreed, then he would throw his hat in the ring with the lovely Margurite!

As the evening and the meal progressed, along with the diminishing contents of the bottle of wine, Paul could see no blot on the horizon regarding this relationship, and therefore decided to treat her with great care and consideration, and relegate his baser instincts to the back of his mind, at least for the foreseeable future!

Margurite felt as though she was walking on air, as she floated through the hall, and upstairs to her room, for this wonderful young man had just kissed her goodnight at the front entrance, and had then jumped in his car and driven away.

During the meal, and as the evening wore on, they had discussed just about every subject under the sun, yet in all those hours he had made no amorous advances, or any remarks of an explicit sexual nature, and she had begun to think, that perhaps the ardour he had shown earlier that day, and the obvious passion he had extolled, were beginning to cool. However, as she stroked her burning cheeks, she recalled, only a few moments ago, he had kissed her three times! And the strength and depth of those kisses, had left her in no doubt of where Paul Cartwright's passions lay!

8

A Wonderful Surprise For Margurite

As summer approached, and it became
obvious that war was imminent throughout
Europe, the authorities decided to evacuate
approximately one and a half million children
from the cities, to less populated safer areas
in the country.

Many children were evacuated from the
tenement blocks near the docks in Hull,
several of them being taken across the
Humber to villages in Lincolnshire, including
Watersmeet.

Rose, being a member of the W.V.S
(Women's Voluntary Service) and a native of
Watersmeet, offered to help, for of course she
knew all the village people, and that local
knowledge would prove to be of inestimable
assistance, in placing the children in their
various billets. Three of the youngsters were
going from the Gables school, so Rose asked
Joan and Enid if Margurite could accompany
her, and help distribute the children.

Margurite was thrilled at the prospect, for
apart from the odd shopping trip into Hull,

she had never travelled far from the school since she arrived. Though her and Paul were now very much in love, and spent every spare moment together, he had been unable to take her on that boat trip up the River Humber as previously promised, because of the pressure of Admiralty work at the shipyard.

The streets of the city of Hull were strangely quiet on that day in August nineteen thirty nine, as the children left, all labelled, and clutching their few personal belongings, enough food for the day, and a square cardboard box containing a gas mask. Many coaches commandeered for the day, and taken off their regular routes, collected the children from the different schools, and transported them to Paragon Railway Station, or to some of the villages in the surrounding countryside, with the exception of the small contingent accompanied by Rose and Margurite.

These were taken down to the ferry, and the obvious pain and unhappiness mirrored in the little faces after leaving their parents, was soon forgotten during the excitement of going on board. The crossing was smooth and uneventful, and even the few known naughty children among them, became overawed and subdued, by this wonderful unprecedented experience. Another fleet of coaches awaited

116

them at the station at Barton-upon-Humber as they left the train, to take them to several villages throughout Lincolnshire.

A smaller bus had been sent to pick up the score or so children bound for Watersmeet, and Rose, assisted by Margurite, separated them from the rest, and shepherded them on board. Finally, amid much excitement, for most of the children had never seen green fields, sheep or cows, in their lives before, the bus came to a halt in the main street at Watersmeet.

As the evacuees spilled out, several villagers who were waiting, stepped forward and began selecting the smartest looking, and those of decent appearance, from the rest, until at last, only two very untidy, grubby little boys were left.

When Rose noticed their unhappy faces, and the lower lip of the youngest begin to curl, her heart was touched, and moving forward she took a small hand in each of her own, and led them away, walking purposefully towards Mill House, with Margurite following closely behind.

As Rose was coming up the road leading to Watersmeet, she had been looking out of the bus window, eagerly expecting to see her beloved mill. Yet when at last it came into view, she had almost cried out in anger and disbelief! For those huge, snow white glorious sails were missing!

Since arriving in the village, Rose had been desperate to discover what had caused her mill to lose it's beautiful sails, and now her step quickened, as she neared her old home. She almost ran round to the rear of the house, dragging the two little urchins with her, and as she rounded the corner of the building, Halle was just crossing the yard.

★ ★ ★

He stopped dead in his tracks when he saw them, but suddenly Rose realised he wasn't looking at her, but at something or someone behind her, and that could only be Margurite, the French teacher!

Time seemed to stand still as they stared at each other, and Rose had the peculiar sensation of being suspended in mid-air, as she breathlessly watched this remarkable scene unfold before her eyes.

After what seemed an Eternity, though actually could not possibly have been more than a few seconds, Margurite dashed past her astonished companion, and cried joyfully 'Pa-Pa! Pa-Pa!'

At the same moment Halle moved forward,

with an expression of undisguised astonishment and joy upon his countenance. 'Margurite! My darling Margurite!' He exclaimed, the excitement and sheer amazement which was coursing through his veins, being reflected in his voice, at this miraculous appearance of his beautiful daughter!

Margurite literally threw herself into his welcoming open arms, laughing and sobbing simultaneously. 'Oh! Pa-pa how wonderful, I had no idea you were here,' her speech was spasmodic, for she was too overcome with emotion to be completely lucid.

He held her trembling body and stroked her satin smooth cheek, then produced a handkerchief and wiped away the salt laden tears, all the while marvelling at her youthful beauty, for Halle hadn't seen his daughter since she was a child, though his estranged wife had sent him a few photographs over the years.

'How wonderful it is to see you Margurite,' he said, finding his voice at last, for the initial shock of seeing her after all these years, had temporarily rendered him speechless. 'Whatever are you doing over here in England Poppet?' He smiled, that had been his favourite name for her, and he'd never used it since leaving the farm in France.

She obviously remembered it too, and smiled with him. 'Oh! Pa-pa, fancy remembering to call me Poppet. You do look very well you know.'

At that moment a tall young man suddenly appeared at the other end of the yard, apparently coming from the orchard which lay beyond. As he approached, Halle stepped forward.

'Ah. I'm pleased you are here son. Richard meet your half-sister Margurite,' he said, turning to the astonished girl.

The young man just stood and stared, then automatically held out his hand, and obviously making a great effort, at last managed to speak. 'Margurite! My half-sister father? Do you mean the one from France?' He suddenly realised he was still holding the hand of this ravishing girl, and with a somewhat garbled 'Pleased to meet you,' dropped it like a hot brick.

At that moment one of the children whose hand Rose was holding, wriggled free and ran down the yard towards the garden, with Margurite in hot pursuit. Of course the laughter which ensued helped to break the emotional tension caused by Richard meeting the daughter of his father's previous marriage for the first time.

When a hot and rather flustered Margurite,

having caught the recalcitrant child, triumphantly returned holding him firmly by the
hand, Rose had a glance at the printed cards
fastened to each of the filthy ragged jackets,
and murmured 'Sam and Ben.' Then turning.
'Right, you Margurite and Richard, take these
two little urchins indoors, put a kettle and
some pans full of water on the fire, strip them
of their filthy clothes, and when you have
plenty of hot water give them both a
thorough scrubbing, then burn the garments.
In the meantime, I am going to visit one or
two old friends in the village, to try and rustle
up something decent for the two boys to
wear.'

When Rose returned an hour later, each of
the children was wearing one of Richard's old
shirts as a makeshift dressing gown. They
were sitting together in a large armchair in
front of the kitchen fire. Rose just stood and
stared open mouthed, unable to believe the
miraculous change that had taken place in
such a short time, to the appearance of these
two children. Their cheeks, though a little
pinched and slightly hollow because of
malnutrition, were coloured and blooming
with health, their hair was fair, shining and
curly, and they were both actually smiling!

★   ★   ★

However, a far greater surprise was in store for Rose, one which she could never have anticipated.

Margurite had been standing by the table, but she suddenly moved forward, and said quite loudly 'Now!'

Immediately the two children jumped down off the chair, and flung open the very large shirts they were wearing. The result was spectacular. For Rose with a stifled scream collapsed in the nearest chair, and for several seconds could only point with an outstretched finger at one of the children, then with an almighty struggle, and in no more than a strained whisper.

'It's a *GIRL!*'

Her companions laughed aloud. 'We know, isn't it marvellous?' gurgled Margurite.

'But their name tags,' cried Rose. 'They distinctly said Ben and Sam. Where are they? Surely you haven't destroyed them?' she said, looking round the kitchen.

'Oh! No, they are here,' said Richard, moving forward and producing the two grubby tattered pieces of cardboard.

'See,' cried Rose triumphantly. 'I knew I was correct. Look Ben and Sam. Now do you believe me?'

'Of course we believe you,' laughed Margurite.

'Richard and I already knew that. What we didn't know, was that Sam is short for Samantha!'

'Samantha,' echoed a bemused Rose. 'But how on earth did you find that out?'

'I told 'em.'

Rose turned to face the origin of that rather eloquent remark. She was still amazed at the transformation that had taken place in the appearance of this tousle haired cheeky looking youngster. Those were the only words Rose had heard him speak since her and Margurite had brought the children to Mill House.

'So, young master Ben. You told 'em. Pllease remember in future to say them, not 'em. I suppose Ben is short for Benjamin, is that correct?'

The little boy stared with a vacant expression at this strange looking lady. He couldn't understand these people. No one had cursed him yet, or even given him a good belting, and he was beginning to worry!

Margurite suddenly stretched out her hand and removed his shirt, then turned the boy round so Rose could see his exposed back. The young tender skin was criss crossed with horrible looking weals, that could only have been caused with a belt or a cane.

Rose gasped in horror when she realised

what this child must have suffered, and involuntarily reached forward, and carefully placing an arm around his shoulders, gently drew the boy towards her.

'Oh! You poor little mite, who could possibly ill-treat a child in this terrible way? Who did this to you Ben?' Rose asked, as she gently replaced the shirt around his shoulders.

The boy was very suspicious and not a little frightened, for he had never known anyone put an arm around him before, and then hold him so close.

'Me mam,' he replied quietly, as though a beating was an every day occurrence, and of no consequence.

A sudden thought struck Rose. 'What about your sister. Has she ever had a beating Ben?'

The boy looked at her, and suddenly he smiled, causing a quite remarkable transformation to take place. He seemed to light up the kitchen with his smile, for now it was possible to see him after all the dirt and grime had been removed, and Rose was astonished to discover that Ben was a very handsome looking boy indeed.

He was slow to answer, but at last he said. 'No, Sam has never had the belt.'

Rose turned to the little girl, she also had

received a transformation. In fact she was almost angelic looking, especially with her freshly washed, beautiful blonde curls, and Rose's heart went out to these two small waifs, who had been thrust upon her because of the impending war, and the inhumanity of man.

'Right, we shall have to do something about you young lady, you can't possibly wear any of these clothes I brought you earlier. Just stay with Auntie Margurite and Uncle Richard, both of you, while I go out again to try and find some suitable clothes for a little girl.'

Upon that remark, Rose turned and left the house, making her way towards a certain cottage she knew of in the village. A moment after she had lifted the brass knocker and allowed it to fall a couple of times upon the solid oak front door, the door was suddenly opened, and a jolly looking middle aged woman stood there.

The laugh lines around her eyes crinkled, and her whole countenance became wreathed in smiles, as she recognised her smartly dressed visitor. 'Rose!' She cried. 'How wonderful to see you. Whatever are you doing here? Please do come in,' she greeted her, as she moved aside.

As Rose stepped into the room, which

opened immediately onto the street, the two women embraced, and held each other tightly for a few seconds, for these two were very old friends and ex-school pals. 'Oh! Alice, it is so good to see you after all this time, and I must say you look extremely well, in fact you don't appear to have aged at all.'

Her friend laughed. 'Well I can assure you Rose, I most certainly have, though if I had spent many more years looking after your Charlotte and her baby Richard, I would probably look much older than I actually am. Sorry, I didn't really mean that the way it must have sounded.'

Rose smiled. 'Don't worry dear. Believe me, I knew exactly what Charlotte was like, and how very difficult she could be. However, I am not here today to discuss the merits or demerits of my late beloved sister. Tell me Alice, are you very busy these days?'

Alice deigned not to reply until she had filled the kettle, placed it on the fire, then prepared a tray containing cakes and biscuits for them both.

'No, not really. What are you after Rose? Do you need someone to take care of Halle and Richard?'

Rose looked upon her friend with a fond, rather surprised expression. 'You are amazing. Yes please Alice I do, though actually it is a little more involved than that. As you are very probably aware, several children have been evacuated from Hull, and some of them are here in Watersmeet. Well they had all been allocated different billets throughout the village, with the exception of two. A boy and a girl, brother and sister. The names on their name tags were Ben and Sam, so naturally I assumed they were two boys. You see they were so filthy and bedraggled it was quite impossible to distinguish a particular gender, and I sallied forth into the village to try and find them some clean suitable clothes, which I did. Of course the problem is, I returned to Mill House in triumph with two sets of boys clothes. You can imagine what a fool I felt, when I discovered that Sam is short for Samantha!'

Alice laughed loud and long at her friend's predicament, then eventually, after drying her tears. 'Here have a cup of tea Rose, and a piece of cake. I think you may need them,' she said, handing over the tea, and then proceeding to cut the cake. 'So, now all you require, is a set of clothes for the girl. Is that right?'

Rose took a sip of her tea, and carefully replaced the cup upon it's saucer. 'No dear, not quite,' she was serious now, choosing her words very carefully. 'I was wondering Alice if you could make yourself available, to move into Mill House to help Mrs.Hill look after Halle, Richard and the two children. I am well aware this is a huge favour to expect from you, but honestly, I just don't know who else to ask. Can you help. Please.'

Though Alice sat perfectly still, her agile brain was ticking over, weighing up the pros and cons of this unprecedented situation. She knew she owed Rose a favour for persuading her sister Charlotte, to employ her as a nanny and housekeeper all those years ago, but this sounded a bit too much. Still, she had nothing else to occupy her time, she might even enjoy it, and anyway, if there was going to be a prolonged war, this could be her part in it, and in later years she would be able to look back and say. 'Yes, that was my war effort.'

She turned to her guest. 'Very well Rose, I will accept your suggestion, if you remember, my sister lives with me and she is quite capable of looking after our cottage while I'm living at Mill House. By the way, how old are the children?'

Rose held out her hands and gripped those of her friend. 'Oh! Thank you Alice. You have no idea what this means to me, I would never have been able to sleep tonight, if I didn't know those little mites were safe. The girl is four and her brother is six. Now they have had a bath and a thorough scrubbing, the change in their appearance is quite remarkable. Sam is a very pretty, fair haired little girl, and Ben is a rather handsome young boy. I appreciate the fact that you are not as young as you were when you came to look after Charlotte and her baby, but I think you will manage alright. If not, then you must telephone me immediately and let me know, so we can make other arrangements.'

Alice agreed with everything Rose had suggested. 'There is just one question I must ask. How on earth did you come to be mixed up with a load of evacuees Rose? Not only that, why have you taken these particular two under your wing?'

Rose smiled, a quiet kind of satisfied smile. 'Well dear, I'm a member of the local W.V.S, and being a native of Watersmeet, naturally I volunteered to help place the children who were being evacuated to this village. Regarding Sam and Ben, they were the scruffiest children of the entire party, absolutely filthy, and when the prospective foster parents had taken the different children of their choice, these two were left standing on their own, you see no-one wanted them. Of course you know what I'm like, and when I saw how miserable, forlorn and unhappy they were, I knew I just had to do something, and that my dear is how I come to be here today.'

Alice collected the tea things, and began moving towards the door. 'Alright Rose, you just sit here and wait a few minutes, while I pop next door to see if I can beg, borrow or steal some nice clothes for your little girl.'

Ten minutes later Alice returned, her arms full of clean beautifully ironed dresses and underclothes for a little girl.

'I say Alice, these are marvellous, whoever gave you all these?' asked an astonished Rose.

For a moment, sadness tinged the countenance of her friend. 'Remember Annie Dixon?'

Rose nodded.

'Well she married Peter Hall, and they had a little girl. Unfortunately the poor child died about three months ago, just before her fifth birthday, and they are both determined never to have another.'

'Do you think I should go next door to thank her, and also offer her some payment? I mean some of these clothes are brand new, as though they have never even been worn.'

'No Rose, I don't think this would be a very good time, she was almost on the verge of tears just now when I left. Now please be patient a while longer dear while I go pack a few things, and I will also bring a case down to put Sam's clothes in.'

Half an hour later they were in the kitchen at Mill House, helping an excited little girl try on her lovely new clothes, with Alice fussing round like a mother hen, and Margurite just as excited as the child.

This was rather a poignant time for the Miller's Daughter, for she had been born, brought up and lived in this house for the first twenty one years of her life, and certain scenes from the past kept tugging at her heart strings, particularly the time she had brought Charles Cartwright to Mill House for the first time. Then the sadness she had experienced at the loss of her beautiful promiscuous sister Charlotte, even though she had so often been in trouble, and had then died so tragically in the mill.

The sound of a car horn interrupted the thoughts of Rose, for she had earlier telephoned Charles and asked him to bring the car round by road, to take her and Margurite home because the bus had left hours ago, and there would be no way of catching the ferry until sometime tomorrow. She flung open the door and greeted him with a kiss. 'Hello darling, sorry to drag you all this way, but I think you will agree it was well worth the journey. Please follow me.'

He followed her into the kitchen, then

stopped dead just inside the doorway. A beautiful little girl was standing in the middle of the kitchen table, wearing very pretty clothes and a charming smile.

Standing beside the table, was a tousle haired, smartly dressed boy, obviously older than the girl. However, immediately he saw Charles he ran across the kitchen to Rose, and with an expression almost akin to terror upon his features, he clung to her skirt, and tried to hide behind her.

'What on earth have you managed to get yourself into this time Rose? Have you started an adoption agency or something I don't seem to have made a very good impression on that young man. Does he only like the ladies?'

Rose laughed. 'No Charles, this is not an adoption agency, just a couple of evacuees from Hull. No-one else in the village would take them, so I thought — well you know me.'

Her husband simply grimaced, but made no reply.

'However, they are here now, and I have engaged my dear friend Alice. Remember Alice?'

The two shook hands and murmured greetings to each other.

'I have engaged her to help with their upbringing. She will also be staying here for the duration of hostilities, if they ever start. Sorry, I haven't introduced the children. The little girl is called Sam, short for Samantha, and her brother is known simply as Ben. Oh! I don't think you made a very good impression upon him because you are a man. I suspect he's had rather a rough time in the past from some members of the human race, if you can call them human. You should see the state of the poor little mite's back. Incidentally, neither of them looked anything like they do now, when they first stepped off the bus. They were both disgustingly filthy, but it really is amazing what hot water, soap and a fair amount of elbow grease can accomplish.'

After Charles had visited the mill, rather painfully because of the memory of Charlotte's untimely death, and walked round the garden and poultry pens with Richard and his father, he and Rose decided the time had come for them and Margurite, to leave Watersmeet and return to Mount Pleasant.

9

Mount Pleasant

Paul was sitting on a window seat, impatiently watching and waiting for the Rolls to appear coming down the drive. When it finally arrived, he leapt up and dashed outside to meet his beloved Margurite.

'Hello my darling,' he greeted her, as he helped her alight from the car. 'Please don't ever do this to me again. I've had a terrible day on my own.'

Margurite chuckled, and drew him to her. 'Oh! Stop thee mithering,' she muttered in the local dialect, which sounded extremely funny, coming from someone with a French accent!

Paul however, didn't seem to notice, he was far too busy trying to reciprocate Margurite's passionate kisses. When at last he managed to surface for a breather, he was able to gasp. 'Margurite! If this is how you greet me after a day at Watersmeet, you may go there again whenever you wish!' Then he added, as an apparent afterthought. 'But only for half-a-day.'

The two lovers had apparently forgotten that Charles and Rose were still sitting in the car, until the sound of the car door being opened, caused them to spring apart.

'I'm awfully sorry Aunt Rose, I had completely forgotten you were still here,' said Paul, trying to hide his embarrassment. 'Please allow me to help you indoors, then I will return Margurite to The Gables.'

★ ★ ★

When Lucy had first taken possession of The Gables, she had quite a large tract of the grounds excavated and filled with water, thereby constructing an idyllic and very attractive lake. She had also built a boathouse with a lovely summerhouse attached.

Now as Paul drove through the gateway leading to The Gables, he suddenly had a wild idea. 'Darling, shall we drive down to the lake, and take the boat out, just for a short trip?'

The ultra quiet engine of the Rolls, the luxurious interior and the smooth ride, had almost lulled Margurite to sleep, and now in her dreamy imagination, she had just been on the verge of giving herself to this wonderful man, whom she had so quickly learned to adore, when the sound of his voice shattered her reverie. 'Did you say something Paul?' she asked, still not fully awake.

He chuckled. 'Yes, now wake up darling and please pay attention. I suggested we drive down to the lake and take the boat out. What do you think?'

★　★　★

Margurite sat up, wide awake now. 'I think that is a marvellous idea. Oh! Paul, may we go for a swim? It is a very warm evening, and I'm sure the water will be warm enough.'

He began to feel the heat rise within, as momentarily he allowed his fertile imagination to run riot! 'Yes, that would be wonderful my sweet, though unfortunately we don't have our costumes with us.'

It was then this lovely girl tentatively made a suggestion, a suggestion which would ultimately change the course of their entire lives!

'No, I know we don't darling. Is that important? I mean, is there any reason why we can't swim without a costume?'

For a long moment Paul sat perfectly still, the silence was almost tactile. His brain was in turmoil, hot blood was racing through his veins. Since that first day, when he had held this gorgeous French girl in his arms in the garden, he had fought successfully against his baser instincts, yet he was well aware of his limitations, and he knew that if they were to go for a bathe in the lake, on this beautiful warm autumnal evening, completely naked, then all his great and good resolutions would come to nought, and would sink to the bottom of the lake forever!

With an effort he jerked himself out of his reverie, she was speaking again.

'Did you hear what I said Paul? May we go for a swim. Please?'

He turned to her, took her in his arms, and though his heart was beating wildly, gently kissed her. 'Yes. My Margurite, we shall go for a swim,' then without another word, he engaged a gear and the car moved silently forward, heading in the direction of the lake.

Margurite had previously visited the lake, but had never been up to the summerhouse. Now as Paul parked his car at the rear of what appeared to be a bungalow, she opened her door and stood on the grass, waiting for him to come round to her side of the car.

Taking her by the hand, he led her down to the lakeside, she gazed at the tranquil scene which unfolded before her. The water was absolutely calm, not a single ripple disturbed the glass like surface.

'Oh! Paul,' she murmured, as she clung to

him. 'How beautiful. Where can we undress darling?'

To say he was astounded by her words, would be an understatement. However, realising that tonight he would make love to this lovely girl, he made no comment, and once more taking her by the hand, led her up the bank towards the summerhouse. Bending down, Paul retrieved a key from beneath a stone, and opened the door.

Margurite emitted a childlike cry of delight, for this retreat was beautifully and luxuriously furnished, with large deep sofas and big comfortable looking easy chairs, complete with huge coloured cushions tossed haphazardly upon them.

'Paul, this is a wonderful setting for lovers. Why haven't you brought me here before?' she asked, her voice almost a caress.

He knew this was going to be difficult to answer, and consequently hesitated.

'Darling. I'm waiting,' she murmured silkily.

'All right, I will tell you. Because my dear, I knew if I brought you here, owing to the lavish furnishings and the incomparable seductive surroundings, we should inevitably make love! Even though that is what I desperately wanted, I was afraid that if I overstepped the bounds of gentlemanly conduct, I may have lost you, and I wasn't prepared to take that risk. You see, to put it simply my darling, I just couldn't live without you!'

She placed her arms around his neck, and gently drew him down among the soft cushions upon the largest sofa, then hurriedly, and with a kind of frenetic haste, began to rip off her clothes, encouraging Paul to do likewise, and in seconds they were both as naked as the day they were born!

That night, in the summerhouse by the lake at The Gables, (probably with the ghosts of Lucy and her daughter Ruth, enviously watching them) the two lovers lay together, and Paul Cartwright attained sexual satisfaction, the heights of which he had never previously experienced, even with Emma, the erotic, exotic daughter of the late, wonderfully sensuous Charlotte.

When the two lovers had finally assuaged their mutual sexual appetites, and Margurite had calmed his trembling perspiring body, he turned to her, and almost in awe as his eyes washed over the length of her naked glorious figure, he spoke, barely above a whisper. 'Thank you, my beautiful darling, that was wonderful, beyond compare, and yet the strength of your passion almost overwhelms and frightens me a little, but perhaps I shall become accustomed to it eventually!'

She stroked and caressed him, until once more his loins began to stir, and as the heat rose within him, he again capitulated to her many and varied repertoire of sexual titillation.

This time, unbelievingly, was even better than the first, and as they finally parted, Paul was utterly drained.

Margurite knew there would be no further response from her lover that night, and with an ecstatic audible sigh of complete contentment, she reluctantly removed her hands from his heaving body, kissed him, then stretched luxuriously among the soft, expensive cushions littering the sofa.

At last Paul stirred, and sitting up, looked around. As he did so, he inadvertently touched her naked breast, and being highly susceptible to his touch, she immediately placed her hand over his, pressing down hard. 'Yes please!' she murmured softly.

Paul gently withdrew his hand. 'No, sorry my love, impossible to manage another session tonight. Now I suggest we forget about our swim, and get dressed as quickly as possible.' As he was speaking, Paul moved away from the naked body of this simmering temptress, and on finding his clothes, proceeded to put his words into effect.

'Come along darling, it's time we were going. I've almost finished dressing and it will soon be dark. I have no wish to court trouble with my aunts for keeping you out late you know.'

Margurite stirred herself, and sitting up offered her hands for him to help pull her up off the sofa. Never for a moment, expecting any ulterior motive on her part, Paul reached down, grasped both her hands, and hauled her up to a standing position.

They were very close, her still naked body, glowing with the health and vitality of her youth only inches away, when suddenly she released his hands and flung her arms around his neck, kissing him passionately full upon the mouth, while pressing herself ever more tightly against him.

Paul, realising he had been duped into this position, gently but very firmly removed her arms from around his neck, then just as gently pushed her down upon the sofa again, remarking as he did so, in a voice which he tried to make stern and tinged with authority. 'Now do come along and get dressed Margurite, otherwise I shall never bring you here again!'

Apparently it worked, for she immediately leapt up and dressed herself, almost as quickly as she had removed her clothes earlier. 'Oh No! Dearest Paul. How can you possibly say such a thing, after we have made such wonderful love together, and so recently too?'

She appeared so downcast his heart was touched, and he regretted his previous outburst. He drew her to him and lightly kissed her. 'Sorry Margurite, you know I didn't mean it. I couldn't mean a stupid statement like that, not after the way you treated me tonight. It's just that I don't want to get you in any trouble for staying out late. Remember darling, you haven't been back to the school since early this morning, and I'm sure they will be worried about you.'

She snuggled closer, happy in his embrace. 'Very well my darling Paul, I believe you. They probably are a little worried about me, but you know this is the first time I have been away from that school since the day I arrived, except of course when I went to Watersmeet, so you cannot blame me for enjoying my small taste of freedom or for making it last as long as possible, particularly when I have the company of such an able and ardent lover! After all we are both over twenty one, well; I know I am, and I think you probably are!'

He laughed aloud at her sense of humour, for he had always been given to understand that the French didn't possess any. 'Yes my dear you are quite correct, no-one really has any jurisdiction over our whereabouts or our private lives, and providing we don't cause any trouble to other people, we should be quite alright. Even so, I think we should return if only to keep the peace and your employers and my aunts happy.'

After that last remark, Paul led his beautiful companion to the door, closed and locked it, then holding hands they returned to the car.

As the Rolls eased to a halt below the front entrance to The Gables, Margurite stirred herself, for lulled by the warmth and movement of the car, and an exquisite feeling of utter contentment because of the earlier love making, she had gently drifted off and was almost asleep.

'Where are we?' she asked drowsily, endeavouring to bring her senses to concentrate on the present.

Paul applied the hand brake, turned to her and kissed her. 'Perhaps that will help to remind you,' he replied with a low chuckle.

Now wide awake, she returned his kiss with a long passionate lover's kiss, until he finally had to push her away. 'No! Margurite,' he gasped. 'I'm sorry, but I just couldn't manage anymore tonight. Perhaps in another month's time it might be possible!'

143

She sat back and stared at him. 'In another month's time!' she cried incredulously. It was then she saw the smile upon his lips and the twinkle in his eye. 'Oh! You darling horrible man. For one dreadful moment, I actually thought you meant it.'

Once more she willingly succumbed to those strong loving eager arms, as they indulged in one last kiss, before entering the house.

As they walked down the hall, Margurite noticed a light showing beneath the study door, and taking Paul's hand led him forward. She knocked and entered, Edith and Joan were both sat at the table marking exercise books. They looked up together.

'Wherever have you two been until this hour?' asked Edith in a stern school mistress manner. 'It is well past ten-o-clock, and we were beginning to feel quite worried.'

Paul stepped quickly forward. 'Terribly sorry. All of this is entirely my fault, Margurite returned from Watersmeet some time ago.'

Edith held up her hand. 'We already know that Paul, I telephoned Rose more than an hour ago. What we would very much like to know, is where have you been with our French mistress, since leaving Mount Pleasant?'

Margurite stepped in to have her say, for after all she was involved in this apparent terrible crime, and she couldn't just stand by and watch her lover take all the blame.

'I am very sorry if we have caused you any inconvenience, but you must remember we are both over twenty-one, and anyway most of this is my fault. You see in France a young girl will often ask her lover to take her for a walk in the evening, especially on such a perfect evening as this, and that is exactly what happened tonight.'

The features of her two employers were a mixture of disbelief coupled with varying shades of disgust. Edith tried to speak, faltered and began again. 'Do you mean?' Her voice was too high pitched, she stopped, then had another try. 'Do you mean to tell us, that you two are lovers?'

Paul realised that the beguiling frankness of the lovely Margurite, would quickly stir up a lot of unnecessary trouble for them both, in this highly religious household, if he didn't immediately put matters in a better perspective.

Putting on a brave front and his most winning smile, he faced the two rather irate inquisitors. 'Now please Aunt Edith, and you too Aunt Jean, just try to calm down a little. There is absolutely no need to get all hot and bothered. What Margurite said a moment ago, is just the romantic way the French have of describing such a situation as ours. It was a beautiful evening with a glorious sunset, and when we returned I suggested that instead of coming straight in, we should take a drive down to the lake, then sit in the car and admire the view, and that my dearly beloved aunts, is exactly what we did. Right darling?' he asked Margurite, as he finished speaking.

She flashed him a wonderful smile and nodded admiringly, but the look in her beautiful eyes, was all the thanks he needed.

After kissing Margurite goodnight at the entrance to The Gables, Paul drove away, and sang at the top of his voice all the way home to Mount Pleasant. He parked the Rolls in the garage, then went indoors. Apparently everyone had gone to bed, for the house was in complete darkness.

10

September 1939

The long halcyon days of a glorious summer were at last on the wane, and though Paul and his Margurite had continued to indulge in their sexual activities throughout the summer, meeting several times each week, and often spending evenings and weekends down by the lake boating and swimming, then relaxing in the lavishly furnished surroundings of the summerhouse, no-one at The Gables or Mount Pleasant, seemed to suspect anything out of the ordinary, or even notice how very much in love they were.

Then tragedy struck, a tragedy of apocalyptic proportions, one that would eventually engulf the entire Western world, and a great part of the Middle and Far East!

Just before five-o-clock on the morning of September the first, nineteen hundred and thirty nine, German forces poured over the Polish Frontier. Tanks and mechanised troops stormed ahead at incredible speed, over ground that had been baked hard during that long hot summer.

Supported by screaming dive bombers, a total of more than a million men forced their way into the country, and it was utterly impossible for man or machine to stop them! For on that day the Germans showed to the world, a new devastating and horrifying method of warfare. It became universally known as *The Blitzkrieg!*

On Sunday morning September the third, at eleven-o-clock, British listeners to the wireless, who were tuned in to the B.B.C, were told to stand by for an announcement by the Prime Minister, Neville Chamberlain.

Throughout the nation, families gathered around their wireless sets, there was not a single soul or moving vehicle to be seen on the streets, and at a quarter past eleven Neville Chamberlain came on the air.

In a strained and weary sounding voice, he stated that Britain had called upon an undertaking from Hitler to withdraw his troops from Poland. *'I have to tell you now, that no such undertaking has been received, and that consequently this country is now at war with Germany!'*

★ ★ ★

Only a few minutes later, air raid sirens wailed out across the country, and thousands of people rushed to their air raid shelters. Almost immediately the all clear sounded, and though this had been a false alarm, the population accepted the situation very seriously, for this time there were no celebrations like there had been at the outbreak of World War One.

All the main and public buildings in Hull had sand bags stacked around them as protection against bomb blast, for this being a large port, and within easy striking distance from Europe, the powers that be, expected their city to be one of the main targets of Germany's Luftwaffe.

Unfortunately in the years ahead, this prophecy was proved to become all too tragically and devastatingly true!

Australia, New Zealand, Canada and France also joined the conflict, and nations throughout Europe who were not yet involved became very anxious, even Sweden and Norway who wished to remain neutral, placed all their armed forces on Red Alert!

Margurite being French, was extremely worried, for of course all her family and friends still lived in France, and on that beautiful Sunday evening, Paul called at The Gables to take her out for a walk down by the lake.

They were both very quiet, each occupied

with their own thoughts on this doom laden day. Finally she found it quite impossible to remain silent a moment longer, and to demand an answer to the question which was uppermost in her mind. 'Paul, will you have to go to fight these horrible Germans?' Her words were rushed, and the tone of her voice was a shade higher than usual.

He turned to her, and was surprised by her lack of colour. Taking Margurite in his arms, he tried to sooth her trembling body. 'No my darling, I think I shall be exempt. You see we have so much Admiralty work on at the yard, I don't think they will even allow me to volunteer for any of the services.'

His words seemed to calm her, and she succumbed to his embrace. So they strolled leisurely on towards their favourite haunt, the summerhouse by the lake.

When they eventually reached the door, Paul bent down to retrieve the key. He lifted the stone and felt around. The key wasn't there!

Straightening up, he looked at his lovely companion and placed a finger to his lips, then silently began to turn the doorknob, and very slowly pushed open the door.

The utterly unexpected scene that met the eyes of Paul Cartwright and his stunning French lover, held them frozen to the spot.

For lying completely naked among those luxurious cushions, which they had used so many times, were two perspiring intertwined bodies, just breaking apart as Paul softly closed the door!

The young lady inadvertently turned her head. *'Paul! Margurite!'* She screamed. *'What the hell are you two doing here?'*

The man eased his naked body away from that of his lovely partner, and almost fell off the huge sofa. He snatched his trousers and frantically tried to pull them on, while his highly embarrassed companion held a small item of underclothing in front of her, hoping to hide her nudity.

Quite spontaneously, Paul and Margurite suddenly burst out laughing. 'Oh! Come on Marcia,' he said to the blushing girl. 'Don't worry about Margurite and I, we have been using this place for months. Don't you worry either Eric, I can assure you, your secret is perfectly safe with us, isn't it darling?' he said, turning to the beautiful French schoolmistress.

Eric Teesdale was now fully dressed, and had apparently regained most of his self control. 'Well Paul thank you for that, and whatever the future may bring, at least we four will always remember where we were, on the day war broke out!'

His remarks were greeted with a chuckle from his three companions, but then Paul suddenly stopped laughing. 'Yes Eric that may be, but at least you two will also be able to remember. *What you were actually doing on this day!'*

Margurite gently cuffed him behind the ear. 'Darling Paul, this day is not quite over yet you know!'

Marcia had now finished dressing, and she also appeared to be her usual happy self. 'We shall have to make some arrangements in future Paul, to make sure this never happens again, we really don't need any double bookings, though of course there is a bedroom at the back containing a double bed!' She added mischievously.

Marcia and Margurite had never spent a great deal of time together, for of course their respective professions prevented that. Now however, as they stood for a while outside the summerhouse on this delicious late summer evening, it was amazing how quickly they built up a certain rapport. Marcia had previously visited that same particular part of France where Margurite was born, and if Paul hadn't intervened, it's quite possible the two young ladies would have continued chattering all night.

After Eric and his companion had left, Paul

drew his lovely Margurite down upon the sofa and eagerly kissed her. 'Sorry I had to break up your conversation with my half sister darling, but you know we didn't come down here this evening just to talk.'

Margurite quickly responded to her lover's caress and his kisses, and within seconds they were both as naked as Marcia and Eric had been, less than an hour ago!

Afterwards, as they lay together, she turned to him, and with a twinkle in her eye, she said softly. 'Paul darling, will you also remember what you were doing on the day war broke out?'

★ ★ ★

The following Sunday morning, Rose suggested that Charles should take her, Paul and Margurite over to Watersmeet for the day, her excuse being, she wished to see how the evacuees were progressing. Actually however, the real reason was the fact that when she had visited Mill House last weekend, it had stirred many memories of the past within her, and she wished to visit the cemetery where she had first met Charles, before taking him to Mill House, and introducing him to her beloved, late sister Charlotte! Also to call upon a few old school friends in the village.

A full blackout had now been declared, and cars were only allowed to travel at night using a minimum of light. Consequently Charles had decided to leave early that Sunday morning, in order to give them a whole day at Watersmeet.

The day dawned bright and clear, with a slight autumnal chill in the air, announcing to the populace that the dreaded winter would very soon be upon them. Yet this particular winter and Christmas was destined to be as no other ever had, with the total blackout, rationing, petrol shortage, and many of the husbands, fathers and young men away from home in one of the services, either in the United Kingdom or fighting overseas.

As the big car drew up round at the back of Mill House, Alice came out to greet them, accompanied by two well dressed, rather smart looking children, a handsome boy and a very pretty girl.

As Rose alighted from the car, she was the first to speak. 'Oh! Alice, the children look really beautiful. How on earth do you manage to keep them looking like this?'

Alice beamed her appreciation at the compliment, stepped forward, and the two old friends embraced. 'I don't dear, well not all the time. However, today is a very special day. Have you forgotten Rose?'

The normally smooth brow of the miller's daughter puckered in a rare frown. 'Yes, I must have Alice. Forgotten what?'

Her companion smiled. 'Well I must say, I am surprised. Fancy Rose Thornton forgetting that today is the Sunday School Children's Anniversary, I just can't believe it!'

Rose was almost overcome with shame and embarrassment. 'Of course. It had completely slipped my mind. Please Alice. Please forgive me. If mother and father, and particularly Charlotte had been alive, they would never have allowed me to forget this day.'

She turned to her husband who had just walked round to her side of the car. 'Did you hear that darling? Today is the children's Anniversary, they will all be performing on the platform at our chapel. Remember I told you about it many years ago? Oh! What a wonderful day to come home!'

Charles appeared slightly bemused. 'Yes darling, but this isn't your home, you live at Mount Pleasant now with me. Had you forgotten?'

Rose laughed aloud, thoroughly enjoying her taste of nostalgia, as she looked around at the stable, the yard and everything that reminded her of a happy childhood, spent here in Mill House at Watersmeet.

For though she was here as recently as last

week, because of the two children, there had been no time to reminisce, linger a while in the garden, or even have a quick look at her beloved mill.

'No my dearest Charles, I had not forgotten. Remember when our Charlotte kissed you out here in the yard, for proposing to me, and how you hated it?'

At the distasteful memory, Charles involuntarily rubbed the back of his hand across his mouth, and inwardly shuddered. 'Yes Rose, I remember.'

As Paul and Margurite joined the group, Rose stepped forward and introduced Paul to Alice and the two children.

Alice moved back a pace to enable her to have a better look at this handsome young man. 'My word,' she murmured in something akin to awe. 'It hardly seems possible.'

'What hardly seems possible?' asked Rose.

'Why, to think I used to sit and talk to Paul in the park, when he was a little boy out walking with his mum, and just look at him now. Gosh he makes me feel old.'

Everyone joined in the laughter that ensued, following those remarks made by Alice.

'Don't you worry about it dear,' chuckled Rose. 'We are all in the same boat. It comes to us all in time you know.'

Upon that reply, Alice turned and led the way indoors. 'I think it's about time we all had a cup of tea,' she said over her shoulder.

The children behaved themselves impeccably, and Rose found it very difficult to believe, that they were the same two grubby little urchins her and Margurite had taken pity on only last week, and brought back here to Mill House.

After they had all partaken of tea and buttered toast, Rose suggested that she and Charles take Margurite and Paul for a walk round the village, but then Alice reminded her that the children's service would begin in fifteen minutes, so there would be no time for them to go.

'That's quite all right Aunt Rose,' said Paul graciously. 'There is absolutely no need for you to worry about Margurite and I, we can go by ourselves, I'm sure Watersmeet isn't so big. I don't think we shall get lost. What time do you want us to return?'

Rose looked enquiringly at Alice. 'Well we're having roast pork and Yorkshire pudding, and all the vegetables are prepared, so I should think no later than one-o'clock,' said Alice with a smile.

Quite oblivious of the fact, and completely unknown to either of them, Paul led his beautiful companion past the tall three storey

157

house, which held so much of the Cartwright family history within it's silent slumbering walls. On they walked, until finally arriving at the hill top gate.

'Oh! Look Paul, there's that wonderful maze we have heard so much about,' cried the lovely Margurite, as they walked through the gate, and onto the hill top. Then she stopped, and gazed in wonder. 'Darling, just look at that wonderful panoramic view. It is exactly as your aunts described it to us. The sloping hill side, the confluence of the three rivers, and then the broad rolling acres of Yorkshire, with this marvellous maze in the foreground. Shall we have a go, and try to solve it?' she asked excitedly.

Once again treading in the footsteps of their ancestors, the two lovers commenced to follow the torturous twisting path, which eventually led them to the centre of the maze, and then amid much laughter and merriment, after turning round, of course led them out again.

Sitting on the bank to recover from their exertions, Margurite suddenly placed her arm around Paul's shoulders and drew him towards her.

'Paul darling,' she said huskily, suddenly very serious as she gazed out across the vast distance spread before them. 'If this war continues, and becomes really bad, do you think Hitler will invade these islands?'

Startled, he turned to her. Obviously such a thought had never entered his head. 'No my darling, of course not. The Germans could never reach here. In the first instance they would have to break through your wonderful Maginot Line, and we all know how impregnable that is!'

She seemed completely reassured by his remarks, though in the very near future as she remembered them, the echo would indeed sound extremely hollow!

Savouring this moment of being on their own for the first time that day, Margurite pulled him closer. 'Kiss me Paul,' she murmured softly.

His eyes washed over her beauty, he saw the invitation upon her moist parted lips, his thoughts mirrored in her own beautiful eyes, and with a low cry, he kissed her passionately, and even before he became fully aware of the urge within, he knew exactly what the ultimate end would be!

For Paul had realised some time ago, that he would never be able to satisfy the voracious sexual appetite of this beautiful French schoolmistress! With that happy thought in mind he rose to his feet, held out a hand and helped her to her feet, and together they scrambled down the hill side, towards a small copse.

Of course Paul had no idea, but that was the same small wood, his late aunt, the ravishing Charlotte had taken her new lover Richard Blakeney, one perfect summer's day, many years ago. If only those trees could talk, what a tale they would have to tell!

Apparently the lovemaking was just as glorious as it was in that luxurious summer-house back home, and as Paul commented afterwards. 'It didn't seem to make any difference where they were!'

As they stretched out together in the long cool grass, Margurite gently stroked his heaving body. 'Thank you Paul. You really are marvellous. I can't imagine why Frenchmen think they are so much better at making love, than the men from England.'

'Nor can I darling,' he replied happily. 'I am sure it is a myth, or just a figment of the imagination of one or more of your countrymen, with an obviously oversized ego. Or perhaps suffering from an inferiority complex,' he added as an afterthought.

With an audible sigh of utter content, Margurite snuggled closer to him. 'Yes my dearest Paul, I'm sure you are absolutely right.'

The two lovers, tired after their mutual

exertions, dozed off in a fitful slumber, and another hour had elapsed, before Paul was rudely awakened by the sound of screaming children running around the maze, on the hill top above them.

Wearily rubbing the sleep from his tired eyes, he shook his still sleeping companion. 'Come along darling, time to go. It's almost one-o-clock, and if you remember, dinner will be served at one.'

Still with her eyes closed, Margurite stretched out a hand and stroked his cheek. 'Dinner, did someone mention dinner?' she mumbled, apparently unable or unwilling to lift herself from this dreamy lethargic state. Then casually feeling her way round to the back of his neck, she once again pulled him down, but this time Paul managed to restrain himself from any further sexual shenanigans, and removing her arm, scrambled to his feet, dragging her up with him.

'Darling Paul,' she pouted. 'I thought you loved me.'

'You know perfectly well I do love you Margurite. I also love my Aunt Rose, and while you are out with me, I am responsible for your welfare, and I have no intention of getting the blame for the two of us being late for Sunday dinner.'

'Ah! Now I understand. It is your stomach

you are thinking about, really Paul. How could you?'

He saw the twinkle in her eye, and laughed with her. 'Yes, maybe there could be a modicum of truth in what you say, after all we have had rather a busy morning, and personally I'm famished.'

The children running around that ancient maze, laughing and screaming as they played, the tall trees around them echoing with bird song, a brilliant late summer sun shining from a cloudless blue sky, caused Margurite to pause and reflect. 'Yes. Perhaps there is a war somewhere out there, but at the moment my little world is just about as perfect as it can ever be!'

So, the happy couple, hand locked in hand, made their way up the slight incline to Mill House, never for a moment anticipating the dreadful verbal diatribe which would erupt over the dining table, on that glorious day, and cause the break up of one particular family, possibly for all time!

11

As the two young lovers entered that low ceilinged homely room at Mill House, they were greeted with knowing smiles from Alice, Halle and Richard. Yet no-one could possibly have foreseen the furore that would shortly erupt, and shake this apparently happy family to it's foundations.

When everyone, having disposed of their roast pork and Yorkshire pudding, accompanied with all the usual home grown vegetables, followed by a scrumptious suet pudding, and were at last replete, enjoying a cup of tea, Richard quite suddenly rose to his feet and addressed the assembled company.

'I am pleased you are all here today, for I have something rather important to tell you.' He turned to face his father. 'I know this will upset you dad, and I'm extremely sorry, but this is something I must do.'

'Come on then son, tell us what this all important thing is, for as you can see, we're all dying to know,' said Halle, with a loud chuckle. His laughter was not repeated, not for the rest of that day, nor for many more to come!

Richard took a deep breath, and looking straight ahead, squared his broad shoulders, then quite calmly and choosing his words very carefully, dropped his bombshell! 'I just want to ask Uncle Charles if he will take me back to Hull in the car, when he eventually leaves Watersmeet.'

'Of course he won't. What the devil do you want to go to Hull for?' asked a baffled Halle, beginning to show signs of irritation.

Richard, well aware of what the consequences would be, plunged on. 'Because father, I'm going to join the army!'

He got no further. 'What the hell do you mean. Going to join the army?' shouted Halle angrily. 'I'll tell you now, no son of mine is going over there to fight the bloody Germans, so you can forget all about that stupid idea, and just concentrate on helping me in the mill.'

Richard lowered his gaze and looked his father straight in the eye. 'I'm sorry if that is the way you feel father, but I'm afraid my mind is made up, and no amount of swearing or blustering will cause me to veer away from this. You see all my friends are going from the village, and I would hate to be the only one who didn't volunteer to do my bit.'

Halle, realising his son's mind was made up, decided to try another tactic. 'Yes my boy, all your friends are going to join up, but you must know they have no choice.' His voice was wheedling now. 'For you see Richard, they are being conscripted into the services, while you have a reserved occupation, grinding corn to help feed the nation, and there is absolutely no reason on earth for you to volunteer.'

'That may be father, but this is something I must do. After all, you volunteered for the army in the last war, so I fail to see why you object so violently to my joining up,' he had spoken quietly and calmly, yet with an air of determination not seen before, but his father wasn't beaten yet.

'Exactly! That is the very reason I do object so strongly. Because I was there the last time and saw at first hand what war does to people. It doesn't just kill them you know. Oh! no, it maims them, often quite horribly. Is that how you want to spend the rest of your life, minus an arm or a leg, or possibly both?'

Richard did not waver. 'No of course not,' their argument, sometimes bordering on violence, proceeded as though no-one else was in the room. 'Though your war didn't seem to harm you in any way.'

Halle glanced, first at Rose and then at Charles, but no help seemed to be forthcoming from either quarter. 'Didn't seem to harm me in any way?' he roared. 'You don't know the half of it! I was blown into a shell hole, and stayed there for God knows how long. When I finally crawled out, I had no idea who I was, and I stayed like that for the next ten years! Until eventually in bits and pieces, my memory returned, and later I came back to England. 'The room was silent now, for the memories Halle had stirred, had caused Rose and Charles to take their minds back to that day in the cemetery, at the funeral of her father, when this tall bean pole of a man had suddenly joined them at the graveside, and of how her sister Charlotte had nearly fainted, and almost followed their father into his grave!

There was a definite atmosphere in the room, and Rose always susceptible to any change, was the first to speak. 'Well I'm sorry Halle, but if young Richard has already made up his mind, I don't see what anyone can do about it.'

He turned upon his sister-in-law. 'What the hell would you know about it? You don't have a clue Rose. How am I going to be able to manage the mill and cope with everything on my own?'

Charles stepped forward. 'That's enough Halle,' he said sternly. 'There's no need for you to speak to my wife in that tone,' then turning to the young man. 'Better go and pack if you're coming back with us Richard, we shall be leaving immediately after the service this afternoon.'

His nephew smiled. 'That's quite all right thank you uncle. You see I packed everything I shall need, before going to bed last night.'

Halle, scowling, yet without a word, abruptly rose to his feet and left the room, slamming the door to behind him, while Richard looked appealingly at Charles.

'What can I say or do uncle, to make him see things my way?'

Charles placed his hand upon the younger man's shoulder. 'Nothing son. Just let it go. Time will tell, and I'm sure in the not too distant future, your father will be very proud of you, and will be only too eager to tell the world of your exploits, and of how his son is helping to win the war!'

★ ★ ★

In the early evening, as the big car eased smoothly to a stop beside the steps leading to that great oak door of Mount Pleasant, the doors were opened, and several tired family members stumbled out onto the gravelled drive.

'Thank God we're home,' muttered a

weary looking Rose, using an expression which for her was decidedly out of character. For that verbal battle with her late sister's husband immediately after dinner, had definitely upset her. Even so, she admired Charles for leaping so staunchly to her defence,

Rose had telephoned her housekeeper prior to leaving Watersmeet, to inform her of the imminent arrival of her nephew, consequently a room had been prepared and the bed already aired, before Richard was taken upstairs.

As Rose and Charles lay in bed that night, she turned to him. 'Dear Charles, what a day this has been, I hope we never see another one like it. You know how I hate family arguments, though I must thank you for rushing to my defence so quickly.'

★ ★ ★

He smiled in the dim light, for everyone had been ordered to try and save electricity. 'Personally Rose, I don't think Halle has ever forgiven you for jilting him, or me either for taking you away and marrying you!'

'Thank the Lord you did Charles. I realised today, I could never have lived with that man for any length of time. Yes perhaps you are right, maybe he does still hold a grudge against the two of us. Anyway, let's try and forget him, I've had enough for one day, goodnight Charles,' said Rose, as she leaned over and kissed him, and within a few minutes she was fast asleep.

The following morning Richard was up early and begged a lift into Hull with Paul. In fact he was so early, City Hall hadn't opened, and he just loitered on the steps, waiting. Eventually however, several other young men arrived, all filled with the same patriotic fervour, and another half-hour had elapsed before the doors were finally opened.

When Richard's turn came to be interviewed, because of his love of cars, or any mode of transport propelled by an internal combustion engine, he asked to join the Royal Army Service Corps.

He was accepted immediately after his medical examination, and was ordered to report to Company H.Q. based in Aldershot, within three days!.

★   ★   ★

Following the declaration of war, a weird seven month period, known in Britain as the 'Phoney War' began, for though the nations were prepared for mass confrontation, apparently no-one seemed to be in any great hurry to commence fighting.

However, this feeling of a false sense of peace and security, came to a sudden dramatic and shattering end during the spring and summer of nineteen hundred and forty, as first Denmark and then Norway, France and the Low Countries fell to a new wave of the marauding Nazi hoards. The wonderful Maginot Line about which the French had boasted for so long, proved no obstacle to the Germans, for they simply walked round it!

During May, Cartwright's shipyard received a call from the Admiralty, asking if they could spare any ships, large or small, to help with the evacuation of the British Expeditionary Force from Dunkirk!

When Paul read the message, he immediately volunteered to take the Charlotte Rose on the following morning's tide, and though Charles wasn't particularly enamoured with the idea, he had to admire the raw courage displayed by his son, and offered to help organize the crew and provisions.

When Paul called in at The Gables that evening, he told Margurite of his imminent voyage to Dunkirk.

'I'm coming with you!' was her instant response.

He stared at her. 'That is quite impossible my darling. We just can't afford to take any passengers, only a skeleton crew. You see my dear, we shall need all available space to enable us to return with as many soldiers on board as possible.'

★　★　★

Though Paul thought it rather strange at the time, when Margurite didn't argue, but seemed to quietly accept his explanation.

However, he would have thought very differently, had he seen and recognised the slight shadowy figure that crept aboard the Charlotte Rose, just before dawn the following morning!

Paul was standing on deck during the voyage to Dover, where they had been ordered to report, when a young lad stepped out of a cabin doorway, saw him and quickly turned to retrace his steps.

Paul just spotted him from the corner of his eye. 'Hey! You there. Boy, come here!'

The youth turned again, and head down, with an old cap almost covering his eyes, walked slowly towards his interrogator.

'Who the devil are you boy? This is no job for a young lad you know, for Heaven's sake lift your head and let's have a look at you.' As he spoke, he reached forward and gently removed the youth's cap.

Open mouthed, Paul stood and stared, momentarily transfixed and completely bereft of speech. Finally he partially recovered, and pointing an accusing finger, 'You!' he croaked hoarsely. Then in a more normal voice. 'What the devil are you doing here? I told you not to come!' He was shouting now and the crew were beginning to take notice, and to stare at this unprecedented scene.

Paul saw them, and taking Margurite by the arm, led her rather forcefully below. 'This isn't a game we're playing here you know,' he began, endeavouring to sound angry as they stood facing each other in his cabin, bristling with unaccustomed anger, and possibly a touch of hurt pride, because this slip of a girl had dared to usurp his authority.

'Please believe me, I know this is no game darling,' she murmured politely, sitting on his bunk nonchalantly swinging her legs. 'But you must remember Paul, many of those soldiers waiting to be rescued may be French, and it would be awful if there was no-one there who could understand them and help them in their hour of need.'

He was calmer now, and had to acknowledge the wisdom of her words. 'Very well darling, but you must realise this is no picnic we're going on, and we shall both very probably be killed or badly wounded!'

Margurite leapt off the bunk and flung her arms around his neck. 'Darling Paul, at least we shall be together. I just couldn't bear it if I was the only one left alive, I should die of loneliness anyway.'

His previous spate of anger had evaporated before this unaffected show of her love for him, and he held her close, then kissed her tenderly.

'Alright Margurite you may stay, welcome aboard. However, if and when the shooting starts, you must promise me you will stay below. Understand?'

'Yes, I understand Captain Paul. Please, what is below?' she asked demurely.

Paul was on the point of expounding his knowledge of shipbuilding, in language a landlubber would understand, when he saw the laughter in her lovely eyes, the half smile just hovering around the corners of her inviting sensuous mouth, and he realised she was teasing him.

★ ★ ★

Code named 'Operation Dynamo'. The evacuation of The British Expeditionary Force from Dunkirk, began on Sunday May the twenty sixth, nineteen hundred and forty. It ended on Monday the third of June, and was responsible for the safe return to these islands, of the massive total of nearly **THREE HUNDRED AND FIFTY THOUSAND** men, in an unprecedented armada of mostly 'Little Ships', numbering between nine and twelve hundred!

The whole of this amazing feat of seamanship was carried out under extremely heavy enemy fire, and almost continuous air attack!

With their love, which had survived this horrendous baptism of fire still intact, the two lovers finally returned to Hull, after twice running that gauntlet of German shot and shell, with themselves and the crew miraculously unharmed, though the Charlotte Rose had suffered severe damage to her superstructure, and a shell had pierced her hull, just above the water line!

Because of this, Paul had been advised to return to port, and when the two weary bedraggled figures eventually arrived home, there was no acrimony over the disappearance of Margurite, only ecstatic joy and thanksgiving for her safe return, and when everyone discovered where she had been, both her and Paul were treated like heroes.

Particularly when the newspapers began to

show photographs of the endless lines of British and other Allied troops wading out in chest high water, to board the scores of patiently waiting 'Little Ships'.

Several of the pictures included enemy planes, and vividly recorded in stark detail huge fountains of water, as bombs and shells rained down upon the stricken army!

However, no time could be spared to celebrate the safe return of the intrepid pair, for because of the war, Cartwright's yard, with all others along the river, was working flat out. A great deal of the work was on cargo ships, and included the fitting of a gun on the poop deck, and providing accommodation for the gunners.

Every cargo ship was eventually fitted with it's own gun, and Cartwright's yard was still fitting them when the war ended.

Unemployment was considerably reduced, and in early nineteen forty, Cartwright's yard employed more than two thousand workers, just on ship repairs and gun fitting, and many of the welders and boilersmiths were women!

★ ★ ★

With the conquest of Belgium, Norway and Holland, the German Luftwaffe now had air bases within easy striking distance of the

North of England. This of course included Hull, being only a short distance across the North Sea, and easily accessible by simply following the River Humber.

When the bombers were on their way to other targets, such as Leeds, Sheffield or Bradford, if they encountered bad weather or heavy anti-aircraft fire, they would simply turn around and drop their load of bombs on Hull, on their way home!

Consequently, and owing to it's position, Hull became one of the most bombed cities in the United Kingdom. Yet for some obscure reason this was looked upon as Classified Information, and the actual name of the target was never revealed to the public, and was always published as *A North East Coast Town was heavily bombed again last night!*

A great deal of timber was stored on the docks, and of course as in any large port, docks are always a prime target.

During the early part of nineteen forty, the Germans began using incendiary bombs, and for several consecutive nights the docks were ablaze from end to end. There were very many raids during the whole of March and April in nineteen forty one, but the heaviest and most devastating were on the nights of the seventh and eighth of May.

At the beginning of the first raid,

chandelier flares were dropped suspended by parachute, illuminating the entire city, and of course giving the bomb aimers a perfect target!

More than three hundred high explosive bombs and thousands of incendiaries were dropped on Hull, nearly three hundred people were killed and hundreds more injured.

Many hundreds of houses, factories and warehouses were totally destroyed, and the entire city was a mass of roaring flames. *It was on those two night, our pilots leaving the coast of Denmark, could see the fires burning in Hull!*

Miles, now in his seventy sixth year, stood with his beloved Ruth on the balcony of a bedroom at Mount Pleasant, gazing in awe and trepidation at the burning city.

They could hear the now familiar unsynchronised drone of enemy bombers, the crackle of anti-aircraft batteries, and the thrump-thrump of the bombs, as more death and destruction rained down upon the suffering, frightened and very angry population of their blazing, once favourite city.

On the second frightful, devastating night of these unprecedented raids, Paul was endeavouring to drive home, being very careful to try and avoid the odd huge hole in the road, left by an unexploded bomb!

He was seemingly surrounded by fire. Houses and other buildings were burning and collapsing on both sides of the street, while behind him, the whole of the dock area was again on fire!

A shadow, silhouetted by the fire, suddenly ran out immediately in front of him from a blazing inferno, that only moments before had been a pleasant suburban house. Fortunately he wasn't travelling very fast, and he braked hard, bringing the car to a halt just in time, as the figure seemed to lean against the car radiator, then slowly disappear!

Never giving a single thought for his own safety, Paul leapt out of the car, ignoring the searing heat, the burst hissing water mains, the thunder of crumbling masonry, the racket of the ack ack batteries, the distant earth shattering explosions caused by falling bombs, in fact the whole chaotic mayhem of being caught in the middle of an air raid of gigantic proportions, and rushed to the front of the car.

The body was lying in a crumpled heap on the road, he bent low and turned it over, and as he did so, he emitted a gasp of astonishment, for up to that moment he thought he had almost run over a man, but as he carefully turned the body, his hand had inadvertently touched the firm breast of a young woman!

Paul had no way of knowing if she was beautiful, for her hair was a tangled, lank bedraggled mass of plaster, soot and brick dust, and unfortunately the same applied to the rest of her. Very carefully he picked up the unconscious young woman, and in so doing happened to touch part of the metal bodywork of his car. It was almost red hot!

Quickly realising the danger of his position, he snatched open the rear door, and literally threw the girl on to the back seat, before leaping in and driving away. For he knew, if he had lingered much longer in that cauldron of fire, his petrol tank would have exploded, and very probably killed them both!

This was obviously by far the worst early evening air raid of the war, and as Paul struggled to drive through the blazing shattered streets of this city where he was born, lived and worked, he began to get angry, and shouted and cursed the Luftwaffe and all things German, until at last he realised the futility of haranguing the Germans, and continued his apparently hopeless quest for a hospital.

Having driven to the Casualty Departments of two hospitals, and having witnessed at first hand the terrible suffering and horrendous injuries of many of the casualties, and realising the terrific strain these air raids were placing upon the doctors, nurses and other hospital staff, he decided to head for The Gables, Edith Joan and his lovely Margurite.

As he began to pull away from the blazing city, even right out there in the country he could still easily find his way with the light from the huge fires, for as he looked back, the whole city appeared to be just one massive raging inferno.

Because of the blackout, Paul had suggested to Edith that she had the brick pillars at the entrance to her drive, painted white, to facilitate locating them in the dark, but that certainly wasn't needed tonight, he reflected grimly.

He drew up at the entrance to the school, ran up the steps and rang the bell, then returned to his car. He spoke to the prostrate figure lying on the rear seat, but there was no reply. Apparently she was still unconscious.

'Whatever are you doing Paul?'

He withdrew his head, straightened up and turned around.

Edith, Joan and Margurite, were all standing there, expectantly awaiting his reply. The fires in Hull gave sufficient light for them to make out the body of a young woman, and before Paul could think of a suitable reply, Edith pushed past him.

'What on earth are you doing with a strange young woman on the back seat of your car? Who is she Paul? Is she dead?'

In as few words as possible, Paul explained to his avid listeners, how this rather unpleasant situation had evolved.

'Oh! My poor darling,' cried Margurite, pushing forward and clinging to him. 'You could so easily have been killed!'

'Yes you could,' remarked the more down to earth Edith. 'However, you are here now, and apparently none the worse for your experience, accompanied by a young woman. We shall have to do something about her. Obviously we can't leave her out here all night, just help me get her out of the car.'

★ ★ ★

After helping them carry his inert passenger up the steps, Paul turned to go. 'Terribly sorry, but I shall really have to leave now, they will be getting very worried about me back home at Mount Pleasant. I can't telephone them because all the lines are down. I think the Central Telephone Exchange must have received a direct hit. Hell what a night!'

The two owners of The Gables, with the

help of Margurite, at last managed to deposit their uninvited guest upon the sofa.

'Margurite, please bring a bowl of warm water, some soap and a couple of towels, while Joan and I remove this young woman's dirty torn clothes,' panted Edith, perspiring freely after her unusual exertions.

Though they stripped her naked, bathed her thoroughly, then dressed her in some of Margurite's pyjamas, she never responded to either word or deed.

There was no doubt she was a very lovely young woman, with a perfect figure, and when Margurite came back from the kitchen after returning the bowl of dirty water and the towels, she sat and watched this beautiful piece of feminine flotsam, that had strayed so fortuitously into the path of Paul's car. For they were all convinced, if he hadn't come along and picked her up, she could so easily have been killed on that ghastly never to be forgotten night!

An hour had elapsed since the three began their vigil, and both Edith and Joan were fast asleep. Fortunately however, Margurite was still wide awake, and conscientiously watching for any sign of life or movement from the patient.

Suddenly, and without any warning sign, her eyes flickered open, yet her countenance remained completely devoid of any expression!

She looked around her, at the ceiling, the walls, the furniture, the two sleeping women, and finally straight at Margurite. Yet still her expression never changed or registered even the slightest modicum of surprise!

'Edith! Joan! Please wake up. Our guest has recovered,' cried Margurite excitedly, giving each of them a slight nudge, to add a little weight to her plea.

When they were fully awake, the three of them tried in their different ways to activate some degree of response from this beautiful, yet apparently dead person! She seemed to exactly resemble a sleep walker, her eyes were wide open, and as the man said. '*All the lights were on, but there was no-one at home!*'

After a further hour of unsuccessful attempts at trying to communicate, Margurite and her two older employers decided it was time to retire. They had agreed earlier that their guest should spend the night with the young French schoolmistress, thereby eliminating the necessity of airing another bed. Also they thought Margurite would be much more likely to respond to any change in the patient's condition, than either Edith or Joan.

When Paul left The Gables that night, the sky over Hull was still a bright crimson, continuing to reflect the huge fires burning the length and breadth of the city.

Arriving home he gave Charles and Rose a short, yet vivid account of his experiences on that dreadful night, and as they learned later, there were four hundred and sixty four separate fires, the majority being major outbreaks. Oil tanks were bombed, paint works, churches, schools, mills and hundreds of houses were blasted indiscriminately, and completely demolished.

They remained perfectly quiet, and listened attentively to his heart stopping dialogue of the night's events, though their interest visibly heightened when he began telling them of the strange young woman, and of how he had finally decided to take her to The Gables.

'What a night you have had my boy,' boomed Charles, heartily thumping Paul upon his back. 'Thank God you came out of it alive. It sounds very much to me as if you saved that poor woman's life, if you hadn't come along and found her, anything could have happened to the lass.'

'Yes Paul, your father is absolutely right. You must call at The Gables tomorrow on your way to the yard, and see if she has regained consciousness, and if so, try and discover who she is.'

When Paul left Mount Pleasant the

following morning, he had no premonition of the devastating shock that awaited him! For his mind was too full of the pleasure of seeing his Margurite again, so it is very doubtful if a premonition of any kind, would have given him cause for concern at that particular time.

Margurite had seen him coming down the drive and was standing by the open door, as he stopped his car near the bottom step. Dashing down the steps two at a time, she fell into his willing arms. 'Oh! Paul darling, I'm so pleased you have come. We really don't know what to do.'

He gently but firmly released himself from her almost overpowering embrace. 'Whatever do you mean, you don't know what to do my dear?' He asked quietly.

'I mean, that young lady you brought here last night, eventually opened her eyes and apparently regained consciousness, but Paul darling, she never speaks or even changes her expression!'

Paul's curiosity was immediately aroused. 'Please take me to her. Perhaps I can persuade her to talk.'

Taking her lover by the hand, Margurite obliged and led him up the steps, across the hall and into the sitting room. The stranger was comfortably seated in a chair facing the window. Completely oblivious of an imminent eruption, Paul nonchalantly walked to the front of the chair, looked at Margurite and smiled, then lowered his gaze.

He stood perfectly still as though carved in stone, all colour drained from his face, then lifting a finger, he pointed. He tried to speak, his mouth opened and closed, but no words came. Finally, after several abortive attempts, he succeeded.

'*You!*' He spat out harshly. '*Why the hell had it to be you? Is this some weird macabre trick you are trying to pull, with a view to ultimately wheedling your way back into my affections? Because, if that is the case, I'll tell you now, you don't stand a chance. So you can pack up this bloody play acting, and get back to the gutter where you belong!*'

His colour had returned, and with it an unprecedented fury. He moved a step closer, and for one frightening moment, Margurite thought he was going to strike the unfortunate young woman.

Fortunately, Edith and Joan came into the room just in time. 'Whatever are you shouting about Paul?' demanded Edith. 'Joan and I could hear you from the other end of the school.'

Her words didn't serve to quell his rage, but at least they prevented him from advancing any nearer to the hapless young female sitting before him. She continued to stare at him, with the same vacant lacklustre expression she had displayed since first regaining consciousness last night.

Again Paul whirled round on her. '*Go on. Tell them who you are. You two timing disgusting whore!*' he snarled.

She didn't move a muscle, just continued to stare at him. 'What's the matter? Cat got your tongue?' He turned to the others. 'Has she been like this all the time?' he snapped.

'Yes,' replied Margurite quietly. 'Paul, do you know her?'

He laughed, a high crazy kind of laugh that frightened her and made her shudder, and one she hoped she would never hear again.

'*Know her?*' he echoed harshly. '*I'll say I know her. This my friends, is Emma! My beloved beautiful, wonderful whore of a wife! And to think that last night I very probably saved her useless rotten life! My God, what a bloody fool I am!*'

For a long moment total silence reigned in that sun lit room, then suddenly everyone began talking at once.

'Your wife!' shouted a stunned bemused Margurite.

'Your wife!' Edith and Joan echoed together. 'And last night, you had no idea?'

Edith added, with blatant disbelief in her voice.

Paul turned on her. 'Of course I had no idea. You saw for yourself how filthy and bedraggled she was when I brought her here. It was almost impossible to determine her sex, never mind who she was.'

After the initial shock had hit him, his anger seemed to have partially abated, though it was patently obvious he was still simmering inside. He felt that somehow he had been cheated by this erring wife of his, whom he had hoped never to see again.

Paul realised however, that as his wife, unfortunately Emma was still his responsibility. He turned to Margurite. 'Will you please come with me darling, and help me take my wife to her father's cottage?'

Margurite understandably appeared slightly hesitant.

'Well I don't really know Paul. Do you think I should?'

'Of course my dear. I can't possibly drive and take her on my own. She is obviously suffering from shock, and though she appears quite docile now, it is quite impossible to predict how she will react at any given moment.'

The French teacher could see her lover was desperate, though this was most definitely not a task she relished. On the other hand, she certainly didn't want her lover's wife, separated or not, living under the same roof as herself!

'Very well. Yes of course I will come with you, just help me with her, and we'll take her out to the car together.'

★   ★   ★

Milly was in her front garden when she heard a car stop outside her garden gate. Rubbing her hands on the apron she always seemed to wear, she walked slowly down the path, to discover who her visitors were at this time of a morning.

With surprise in her voice, she recognised him. 'Good morning Paul. What are . . . ?' Milly stopped in mid-stride and speech. For the rear door of the car had opened, and a smartly dressed young woman was helping someone out of the car.

'Emma!' Milly screamed, as she regained her speech and her mobility.

Rushing forward, she brushed Margurite aside and embraced Emma, then holding her hands, she stepped back and looked at her closely. No sign of recognition had crossed Emma's face, or flicker of light illuminated her blank lacklustre eyes.

A baffled Milly stepped closer. 'What's wrong Emma? Please speak to me. This is me, your devoted Milly.' There was still no change in Emma's demeanour.

Milly suddenly turned on Paul. 'What have you done to my beautiful Emma?' she demanded harshly.

Before Paul could reply, Tom Laceby rode up on his bicycle, apparently he used it to save valuable petrol coupons, whilst doing his rounds of the estate.

'Good morning Paul,' he said affably as he leaned his bike against the garden fence. It was then, he saw his daughter. 'Emma!' he shouted joyfully. 'What are you doing here?'

She made no reply, just stared at him with the same blank expression she had worn, since Paul found her the night before.

Her father moved quickly to her side. 'Emma, look at me,' he swung her round to face him. Still she made no movement towards him, or showed any sign of recognition. In desperation he shook her. 'Emma. Speak to me. This is your father. For God's sake say something!' He turned to Paul. 'What's wrong with her? How long has she been like this?'

Paul explained to the distraught Tom Laceby, how his daughter came to be in this extraordinary situation, and of how she had spent the night at The Gables.

'Why the hell didn't you bring her straight here man? You know this is where she would want to be.'

Margurite stepped forward. 'If you are Emma's father, and you think as much about her as you profess, then you should be very thankful that Paul came along last night and found her when he did. She could so easily have been killed in those terrible air raids. In fact, instead of upbraiding him, you should be thanking him, because I think he saved your daughter's life!'

A rather bemused Tom and Milly stared at this beautiful young woman standing beside Paul.

'Very well miss. I have no idea who you are, but I take your point.'

Paul interrupted. 'Sorry Tom, Milly. Please allow me to introduce Margurite, the French school teacher at The Gables.'

'Ah! I thought she was French,' said Tom wryly.

'That's the first time I have ever been told off by someone with a French accent, though I must say, you speak very good English my dear.'

Margurite flashed him a quick smile in return for the compliment. 'Thank you kind sir, though none of this is going to determine what we can do for poor Emma.'

Milly, beginning to think her authority was being slightly undermined, stepped forward and took Emma's arm. 'Please don't worry about it,' she remarked sweetly. 'I'm sure her father and I can cope quite well. Thank you Paul for bringing her home, and now I think we should take her indoors. Come along Tom.'

12

After the horrendous bombing raids on those two never to be forgotten nights in May, the Germans appeared to have discovered other targets for their nefarious operations, for the raids upon Hull became more sporadic, thus enabling the populace to evolve some kind of order from the utter chaos and wanton destruction left by the enemy.

★ ★ ★

In the meantime however, Emma though fit and healthy, and still very beautiful, never seemed to take any interest in anything. She continued to maintain the same lack-lustre look, she had worn when Paul found her on that terrible night.

As the days lengthened and the weather improved, Tom with Milly's blessing, allowed his daughter to leave the cottage and go out for long walks on her own.

Out there in the peaceful tranquillity of the English countryside, on a beautiful summer's afternoon, no-one could possibly have imagined what fate lay in store for this lovely girl, apparently still suffering from the shock of that fateful night!

★   ★   ★

Tim Carter, even after all these months, was still simmering from the indignity of being ejected so unceremoniously through the back door of the Cartwright household at the instigation of Marcia, and he had vowed that at the first opportunity he would somehow wreak his revenge upon the Cartwright family!

For of course, after that debacle at Mount Pleasant, Tim had immediately been told in no uncertain terms, his services were no longer required at Cartwright's shipyard, and when he had tried for employment at other yards along the river, he soon discovered his reputation had preceded him.

Because of the impending war, the fact that no-one would employ him, and most of his friends had already joined up, Tim had decided the army was the best solution to all his problems.

He was now on a ten day embarkation leave, this was his second day at home, and as he looked out of his bedroom window and saw what a glorious day this was going to be, he had a sudden desire to revisit the

Cartwright Estate, and wander along some of the lanes and by-ways he had travelled so often in his youth.

Knowing he would not be made welcome if anyone saw him, Tim had hidden his borrowed motorcycle in a small copse, and was now enjoying the fresh air and beauty of the surrounding countryside as he wandered along one of his old favourite walks.

Suddenly Tim stopped dead in his tracks, then hurriedly slipped behind the nearest tree, for walking slowly towards him was a young woman.

She hadn't seen him, and hardly daring to breath, Tim waited. He almost cried out when eventually he recognised her. Allowing her to draw level, Tim at last stepped out into the lane.

'Hello Emma!'

If Tim Carter had expected a scream or some other form of violent reaction from this lovely young woman, he must have been very surprised, for she just slightly turned her head and glanced calmly in his direction, then continued on her way!

Remembering the embarrassment and the indignities he had suffered at the hands of this family, and also remembering the good time he and Emma had enjoyed in the shower on that day of the tennis match, coupled with the heat of this summer's day, and Emma's beauty, Tim realised with some relish, there could only be one satisfactory outcome to this totally unexpected meeting.

Moving quickly forward, he caught her up and reached for her hand. 'Not so fast Emma,' he said, as he turned her towards him.

She made no response, either by word or flicker of recognition, just gazed up at him, with a dead lack lustre look, in her once beautiful eyes.

To say Tim was bewildered would be putting it rather mildly, for he had never been faced with a situation quite like this.

However, Tim having some kind of a dubious reputation to uphold where the fair sex were concerned, and still carrying this chip on his shoulder regarding the Cartwright family, decided to go ahead as normal, whether Emma liked it or not! For after all, this was his last leave before going abroad, and he may never get another opportunity like this, in fact he may not live to see this damn war through to the end!

All this had flashed through his brain in a few seconds, and now with these thoughts in mind, he gave a quick glance up and down the lane, before leading Emma to a small wood, then taking her in his arms, he kissed her.

Tim, being Tim, was not surprised when Emma didn't object, for the size of his ego was so gigantic, he thought all women should behave like this when he kissed them! However, much to his chagrin, she didn't respond to his kisses, there was no return kiss, no warmth, no hug, nothing. It was like kissing a dummy in a shop window!

This total lack of response from the silent Emma failed to cool the ardour of Tim, and throwing all caution to the winds, he removed his trousers, taking them off completely, as he remembered that other time, on just such a day as this, when Marcia had leapt up and ran off, leaving him struggling with his pants round his ankles. 'That won't happen today,' he muttered grimly.

He lay the suppliant Emma upon a patch of soft grass, and proceeded to remove her clothes, until finally she was completely naked. Gazing down upon the beauty of her, he realised what a wonderful body she possessed, and thought how lucky he was, yet thinking at the same time what a waste, for she didn't appear to have any interest in anything, either in him or whatever he did to her.

Suddenly, halfway through the lovemaking,

Emma came alive, she screamed, then as she entwined her limbs around his naked body, she moaned in ecstasy as she drove her nails ever deeper into the flesh of his broad back!

Tim Carter never discovered why Emma had behaved in such a weird manner when they first met, but whatever had been the cause, he was convinced he had been the cure!

When they parted a couple of hours later, Emma had still never uttered a word, though Tim was sure she knew what he had said to her, anyway he would know tomorrow, for he had told her to meet him at the same time, in the same place.

As Emma walked leisurely home in the heat of that late afternoon, she smiled, and almost unconsciously began to hum an old song to herself, for during those exciting, hectic wonderful few moments she had lain with her lover, her mind and body had become rejuvenated, and as the old juices began to flow, odd bits of her memory had returned!

However, for reasons best known to herself, Emma decided to continue with her charade of silent inadequacy, for she was well aware of Paul's obsession for the beautiful French school mistress, and she knew he would never dare divorce her while she was in this blatantly obvious mental state, brought on by that horrific night of the air raids.

* * *

'So you did understand what I meant yesterday,' said Tim, as Emma melted into his embrace, and willingly offered her sensuous mouth to his.

For the rest of Tim Carter's leave, every day the two lovers continued their passionate illicit affair, and though Emma had only emitted the occasional low moan, or squeal of ecstasy during these shenanigans, she had never spoken a single word, until they were parting on Tim's final day, for he had to report back to his unit the following morning.

He held her tight, and kissed her for the last time. 'Goodbye Emma. It was really wonderful meeting you again. This must have been the best leave any soldier could possibly have had. I hope I haven't left you with a little Carter, that would really put the cat among the pigeons!'

To Tim's amazement, Emma looked up at him, gave him a ravishing smile, and cooed in a voice which could only be described as a caress. *'I do hope so darling, that would be wonderful!*

With that remark, she removed her arms

from around his neck, gave him one last peck upon the lips, turned and fled across the fields, heading towards home.

As though cast in stone, Tim Carter stood and watched her go, utterly bewildered. She had met him every afternoon for the last nine days, and they had made wonderful love on every day, occasionally several times, and not once in all that time had she ever said a single word.

Yet now, as they were parting, she had spoken. It wasn't only that, it was the words she had said!

Now Emma had disappeared below a slight rise in the land, and Tim shook himself back to reality, and as he began to retrace his steps towards his machine, he suddenly laughed, and shouted aloud. 'Well if I have left a little something with our Emma, that should do as a small deposit towards settling my account with the Cartwrights!'

13

One lovely Saturday morning, approximately six weeks after Tim Carter had returned to his unit, Paul had driven over to The Gables and had suggested Margurite accompany him, for she was quite an accomplished artist, and had often mentioned a desire to do a water colour of Mount Pleasant. Also his father hadn't been well recently and had stayed at home for the past week, and because of this Paul had brought several important business documents home for them to discuss together.

Never wanting to leave Margurite alone, particularly at week-ends, he thought this would be a wonderful opportunity for her to sketch and probably paint her copy of the house.

The French mistress had agreed immediately to her lover's suggestion, and now she was sitting beneath the shade of a lovely chestnut tree on a fold up chair, with her easel firmly placed in front of her.

Margurite had completed her sketch of the house, including that glorious dome, and was on the point of applying the first touch of blue for the sky, when she suddenly sensed someone very close behind her, quickly turning her head, Margurite emitted a gasp of amazement, for Emma was standing there!

However, that was not all. She was smiling! But this was no smile of welcome. This was a smile of pure malevolence, laced with hatred, for she had inherited all the cunning and evil from her mother, the beautiful wicked Charlotte, and was now about to manifest how bad she really was. '*So, you are the whore who has stolen my husband!*'

The words came out as more of a hiss from a snake, than a human being, albeit a beautiful one.

Margurite leapt from her chair and shrank back, almost knocking her easel to the ground, more from the shock of Emma speaking, than from the words she had uttered, for this was the first time the French mistress had heard her speak since the night Paul had taken her to The Gables.

Drawing upon untapped reserves of strength, she faced the wife of her lover. 'So. You can speak. When did you regain your power of speech? Does anyone else know? Or is this just our little secret?' Margurite asked, her voice dripping with sarcasm.

'You'll sing a different tune when I've finished with you, you bitch!' Emma shot back. 'Now I haven't come here today just to waste my time talking to the likes of you. I have something rather important to tell you.'

'What can you possibly have to say that would be of the slightest interest to me?'

Emma gave out that horrible witches cackle, and involuntarily Margurite shuddered. *'Yes, you need to go pale and look scared. No-one else knows about this but I am six weeks pregnant!'* She paused. If the pause had been for effect, it certainly worked, for Margurite immediately sat down again, but not for long.

Again Emma smiled, if one could call it a smile. 'That is not all, you haven't heard the best bit yet. The father is Eric Teesdale, you know, that wonderful man Marcia married! That snippet of information is just for you and I, though of course there will be no point in you telling anyone, they will never believe you. For you see, you are the only person on this earth who knows I can speak again! *So far as the rest of the world is concerned, the father of my unborn child is my beloved husband, Paul Cartwright!'*

★   ★   ★

As Rose happened to glance out of an upstairs window, she saw the figure of a woman disappear behind some laurel bushes on the edge of the lawn.

Then she lowered her gaze. 'Paul! Paul!' she screamed.

From the bottom of the stairs. 'Whatever is the matter?'

By this time Rose was on the landing looking down. 'Paul darling, something is wrong with Margurite. She is lying on the grass quite still!'

Paul tore out of the front door and across the lawn, shouting 'Margurite! Margurite!'

Finally he reached the inert body of his lover, and taking her in his arms, he spoke her name, over and over again. At last, much to the relief of an agitated Paul, her eyelids fluttered open and as she gazed up at him, he saw an amalgam of horror and disbelief lurking there.

'What is it my darling? What has upset you? You look as though you have seen a ghost.'

She clung to him, and tried to speak, but no words would come. She tried again, and again. After several unsuccessful attempts. 'Oh! Paul darling. It was horrible. I didn't know she could speak. She said she is pregnant, and that the father is Eric Teesdale, but she is going to tell everyone the child is your's!'

Margurite was babbling now, almost

incoherently, sometimes in English, sometimes in French, and a bewildered Paul was
almost at a loss to know how to cope on his
own, when a hand was placed gently upon his
shoulder.

'Come along darling,' said Rose quietly.
'Help me take her indoors, then you can pour
her a stiff brandy.'

Some moments later they were sitting in
the comparative coolness of the oak panelled
library, Paul next to his lover, watching her
intently as she sipped her brandy, and he gave
an audible sigh of relief as her colour
returned.

'Now my dear, please tell us what actually
happened out there this afternoon.'

After telling them her unwelcome visitor
was Emma, she then reiterated what she had
said previously, only this time a little slower,
and much more articulate.

Much to Margurite's concern, Paul
appeared quite sceptical. He actually smiled.
'I say old girl, all this sounds a bit
far-fetched. Are you sure you didn't just nod
off in the afternoon sun, and have a dream
or an hallucination or something?'

For the first time since they had met,
this lovely French girl, suddenly showed a
flash of temper. 'No! Of course I didn't.
Don't talk so bloody stupid Paul! Do you

really think I could dream up something as unpleasant and evil as this, and then tell you about it?'

He looked stunned by her outburst, she had never spoken to him like that before, in fact he had no idea that his beautiful lover possessed a temper.

'I'm terribly sorry my darling,' he said placatingly. 'Though you must understand my scepticism. As far as anyone else knows, Emma has never regained her speech since that terrible night of the air raid.'

Perhaps his quiet tone had helped to soothe her, for she appeared much calmer now, though when she spoke he could tell there was still an undercurrent of irritation in her manner towards him.

'Yes, that is exactly what she said.'

'What do you mean darling? Exactly what she said?'

'Emma said, no-one would believe me, because I am the only person on this earth who knows she can speak!'

★ ★ ★

Rose moved uneasily in her chair, as she thought of Charlotte her late sister, and Emma's mother. '*Dear God, please don't allow Emma to be like her!*' She had spoken

206

in no more than a whisper, more to herself than her companions.

Paul turned quickly. 'What did you say.'

Rose averted her eyes, then looked out the window. 'Nothing dear, I was just thinking aloud. You know we may all be worrying unduly over what Emma told Margurite. She might not even be pregnant. She may be saying all these things out of jealousy, and simply to stir up trouble between you and Margurite, also Marcia and Eric.'

Though Rose had tried to sound convincing when she made these statements, a small niggling doubt still persisted at the back of her mind.

As no-one else spoke, Rose continued. 'However, I think it will be better for everyone if we say nothing at the moment, just wait and see if Emma really is pregnant.'

Paul turned to her. 'And what if she is? What happens then, particularly if she makes these ridiculous accusations?'

Rose endeavoured to calm him. 'I don't think she will darling. You see, to enable her to accuse anyone, she will have to let it be known that her power of speech has returned, and somehow I don't think that is part of her plan.'

Her companions seemed to have accepted this solution, and Rose offered up a silent prayer of thanks, though she knew in her heart this was only temporary, and shuddered to think of what may very probably be the outcome of this afternoon's fiasco.

★ ★ ★

One Sunday morning, a couple of weeks after Emma had visited Margurite on the lawn at Mount Pleasant, she was sitting down to a breakfast of eggs and bacon with her father and Milly.

'Come along Emma,' said Tom. 'Why are you just tinkering with that bit of bacon. Good Lord you know we aren't allowed much because of the rationing, if you don't really want it, pass it over here.' As he finished speaking, he reached across the table, and she gladly gave him her entire breakfast!

Milly watched this episode unfold before her eyes with a great deal of trepidation and disbelief, but decided to say nothing until later.

That night after Emma had gone to bed, Milly turned to her husband. 'Just put your paper down Tom, and please listen very carefully to what I have to say.'

Tom looked at his wife in some surprise, for it wasn't very often she spoke to him in such a serious vein. He obediently folded his paper, placed it upon the table, and proceeded to fill his favourite pipe. He smiled through the smoke as he looked at her, completely unprepared for the devastating bombshell she was about to deliver. 'Yes my dear. What is it?'

Milly never had been one to beat about the bush, she would never use ten words if five would do the job just as well. She looked him straight in the eye. 'I believe your daughter is pregnant!'

Apart from the noise Tom's pipe made as it fell from his open mouth, the silence in that room was almost tactile, his colour heightened, then paled. At last his vocal chords began to work. 'What the hell do you mean woman?' he shouted. 'Don't talk so bloody stupid, she never goes out anywhere.'

'Well I think she is, and if so, she hasn't got like that through sitting on the privy!' Milly's tart reply was tinged with fury, for this was the first time he had spoken to her like that.

'If you remember, some weeks ago you allowed her to go out for long walks on her own, I remonstrated at the time, but you took no notice, and neither of us has any idea where she went, or whom she met, and if she can't talk, how on earth are we going to find out?'

Tom had no answer to that, and after

retrieving his pipe, he refilled it, sat hunched forward and pulled furiously upon the stem, creating huge clouds of impenetrable smoke, until finally Milly coughing and with her eyes running, had to leave the room.

The next morning Tom sought permission to take Emma in the car to Hull.

'Is this journey really necessary?' asked Paul. 'I'm just going to the yard myself, and I could easily take her.'

'Yes, I'm sorry Paul, it is very necessary. I'm taking your wife to see a doctor!'

Paul immediately gave Tom permission to take the car, though he didn't ask the reason why Emma needed to visit a doctor, he dare not, for he thought he already knew!

Milly's worst fears were verified on that visit to the doctors, yet she still found it very difficult to believe. When they were back home and Tom had gone out to his work as supervisor on the estate, she and Emma were alone.

'What the hell were you playing at, you stupid stupid whore! I thought you told me you couldn't have any children because something went wrong with the abortion. Well obviously it didn't. Who the hell is the father? Or don't you know?'

The pathetic way Emma looked at her, caused Milly's heart to soften, for she had brought up this beautiful young woman, almost from childhood, virtually on her own, yet she knew a firm hand was desperately needed here. Fighting back an almost overpowering desire to take the lovely Emma into her arms, and hug and comfort her, Milly pushed a piece of paper and pencil across the table.

'Write his name down. Now!' She had spoken as harshly as she could, yet she knew it had sounded rather pathetic.

Emma picked up the pencil, put the end in her mouth and began to chew it.

The room was hot and oppressive, and the silence was absolute. Finally, Milly snapped, she could bear the tension no longer, she reached over the table, and snatched the pencil from Emma's mouth. 'Write his name!' she screamed, as she flung it down upon the table. 'For God's sake, write the name of the man who defiled you!'

With the same uninterested, lack lustre look in her once beautiful eyes, the late Lady Emma Brackley, now Emma Cartwright, took the pencil, turned the paper towards her, and forming her letters very carefully, she wrote in large capital letters *MY HUSBAND PAUL CARTWRIGHT!*

An impatient Milly reached over and snatched the paper almost before Emma had finished writing. Turning the missive round, she gave a low scream, then sat perfectly still as though turned to stone.

No words could describe the feelings churning around inside Milly's mind that day. Her first feeling was one of hate and revulsion for this man who had dared to have his way with her beloved Emma, particularly after the way he had treated her, for even now he was probably with his French mistress!

Then another feeling would take over. One of thankfulness, that at least the man was Emma's husband, albeit an estranged one, and not some tramp or farm worker who had accosted her during one of her long lonely walks.

As Emma went to lie down for a rest after rather an exhausting morning, Milly sat back in an easy chair, and wondered what devastating repercussions there would be when all of this became public knowledge.

14

On the weekend following Emma's visit to see the doctor, Paul had again brought his lovely Margurite to Mount Pleasant, and after going to church, and then partaking of a scrumptious Sunday dinner of roast beef and Yorkshire pudding. While other members of the family were relaxing, some of them sleeping, the two young lovers were strolling around the gardens, in the warm summer sunshine.

They were both so totally engrossed in their animated conversation, neither of them noticed Tom Laceby until he stepped out from behind a shrub immediately in front of them.

'So, Mister Bloody Paul Cartwright! How the Hell are you feeling today? All happy and content with your new mistress, you lousy two timing bastard!'

Before Paul could even think of a suitable reply to this malicious outburst, Tom lunged forward intending to catch the unsuspecting Paul with a vicious blow to the head.

However, quite unknown to Tom Laceby, Charles had taught his son the rudiments of boxing, though the real art of fighting he had taught himself in the rough and tumble of working in the shipyard, where no boss or person in authority worth his salt, could expect to gain any respect or discipline among the men, if he was unwilling or unable to use his fists.

Today that hard school of learning served Paul well, for the blow his opponent had aimed, sailed harmlessly by, as much to the surprise of Tom, he neatly sidestepped, and delivered a hard right uppercut to the ex-guardsman's jaw, the unexpected result being that Tom was knocked flat on his back in a vegetable patch.

He struggled rather unsteadily to his feet, mouthing obscenities. 'I'll kill you. You young — !'

Tom got no further with his tirade, for he was cut off in mid-speech by another vicious blow, and once again joined the cabbages, only this time Paul actually stepped forward and helped the older man to his feet.

He tried to shake off the grip upon his arm, but Paul was adamant. 'Now come along Tom, don't be stupid, I could carry on knocking you down for the rest of the day, if that is what you want. Whatever your problem is, I'm sure there must be a more civilised way of settling it than this.'

Tom, in some embarrassment, wiped his bloodied mouth on his shirt sleeve, and stared askance at his young adversary. 'You don't know, do you?'

Paul pretended to appear puzzled. 'Sorry Tom. I'm afraid you've lost me. Know what?'

Tom gazed out across the gardens and the lawns, his face expressionless, then slowly he turned to face the target of his anger, and in a cold hard voice he spoke. 'You dirty philandering little bugger, my Emma is pregnant, and she has written down that you are the father of her unborn baby!'

For a full twenty seconds, which seemed to stretch to Eternity, apart from the continuous caw-caw of the rooks high in the elms lining the drive, no other sound broke the stillness of that warm afternoon.

It was then this beautiful, elegant French schoolmistress, suddenly came alive, and caused the two men to whirl around and gaze in awe as she verbally tore into Tom Laceby.

'You silly stupid bloody moron! I understand you have a saying in England. Do not shoot the messenger. Well I agree, shooting would be far too good. You deserve to be horse whipped! You must be terribly naive if you believe everything your slut of a daughter tells you!'

Tom lunged toward hie beautiful inquisitor, but Paul leapt forward and barred his way. 'I wouldn't even try if I was you. Until now I have been quite gentle, but if you continue to push me, I shall turn really nasty.'

The words were spoken very softly, the tone almost a caress, yet Tom, who as an ex-guardsman had faced death in many situations without fear, saw it again that day, lurking behind the cold eyes of Paul Cartwright, and he backed down.

After that interlude, Margurite continued.

'Approximately two months ago, your beloved Emma came up behind me as I was sitting on the front lawn of this house, and spoke to me.'

Tom made as if to interrupt, but she brushed him aside.

'She told me then that she was pregnant, and that Eric Teesdale was the father, though she was going to blame Paul.'

This time Tom did succeed with an interruption. 'How can you stand there and lie to me like that? It just goes to show you will go to any lengths to get your filthy lover off the hook. Both of you know perfectly well, my Emma has not spoken a single word since the night of that damned air-raid, and I really find it very difficult to believe that you are saying these things, or that you

216

condone them Paul. However, I shall certainly have a word with Eric Teesdale when I see him.'

Paul actually smiled. 'I think you may find that a bit of a problem Tom. Obviously your daughter didn't know, or if she did it had completely slipped her nasty little mind. You see Eric joined the army several months ago, I thought you knew that.'

For the first time Tom Laceby appeared slightly ruffled, his temper had cooled and his abrasive manner had disappeared, but then he had another thought. 'Yes of course. I knew that, but this is just another lie that you two have made up, so Eric doesn't come into the picture anyway.'

Seeing Tom's discomfort, again Paul smiled. 'Well I think he does. If I knew that Eric was in the army, which of course I certainly did. Why on earth would I invent such a cock and bull story as this? No, I'm sorry Tom, but you are going to have to sit down and have a very serious talk with your daughter, and while you're talking, please don't forget to mention that ominous word slander! Also, that the cottage goes with your job, and during a war, isn't a very good time to be without a roof over your head!'

Following those remarks, a very disillusioned and rather subdued Tom Laceby, brushed past the two lovers and returned to his cottage.

* * *

Milly and Emma were almost asleep, relaxing in deck chairs in the garden, sitting beneath the shade of an old apple tree, when they were rudely awakened by the loud banging of the garden gate. They both looked up, startled, but when they saw the expression on Tom's face, they knew that someone was going to be in deep trouble.

'Inside, both of you,' he said curtly, as he strode past the now wide-awake women.

Without a word, they got up and followed him into the cottage and straight through to the sitting room, where he motioned each of them to a chair, while he continued to stand and pace the floor.

He walked the length of the room twice, then suddenly turned on Emma. 'Right young lady. No more silly bloody games! How long have you been able to speak? When did your voice return?'

Tom raised his hand to strike his beautiful daughter, and thought better of it as Milly screamed, though Emma never flinched. She still continued to gaze out upon the world with that same blank vacant look.

Realising the hopelessness of his task, Tom turned to Milly, and with a break in his voice, he asked. 'What are we going to do? I have just been talking to Paul and his French mistress.'

He then proceeded to give them a resume of the recent conversation that had transpired in the gardens of Mount Pleasant, being careful to omit the part when he was knocked flat on his back in the vegetable patch by Paul, the very man he had gone to confront regarding Emma's pregnancy.

Though Milly remained silent during the whole of Tom's narration, she was literally seething inside.

Finally, he stopped talking.

Now it was her turn to stand, and to pace the room, as Tom sank into her vacant chair.

She turned on him, her hackles rising, her eyes flashing. 'And you believed all that tripe? My God Tom Laceby, you're not half the man I thought you was. Why the hell didn't you thrash the philandering fornicating bastard. You say that French piece reckons Emma spoke to her, why she must be just as bad as he is. Still I suppose she has to be, for of course she will be well aware which side her bread is buttered. Well I'll tell you now, I'm not going to stand by and let them get away with this, somebody is going to pay for

what has been done to my Emma, we
certainly can't afford to bring up one of Paul
Cartwright's brats. So you had better put
your thinking cap on Tom Laceby, before I
take the twelve bore to the mighty Paul and
his flibberty gibbet of a French Mistress!'

Emma sat perfectly still, never batted an
eyelid, and said absolutely nothing, though
deep within, she was literally hugging herself
with glee!

15

Fortunately, none of the fantasies Emma had expounded to Margurite that day on the lawn at Mount Pleasant, caused any friction between the French Mistress and her lover Paul Cartwright, for she knew she could trust Paul at all times, and anyway, Emma had said Eric Teesdale was to blame for her condition, and later that was also proved to be a falsehood.

Bearing all this in mind, Margurite had come to the conclusion that the estranged wife of her lover could not be trusted. Even now, she was still keeping up this stupid charade of being dumb, though Margurite smiled to herself, as she wondered how long Emma would be able to sustain her inability to communicate, once she went into labour!

One Saturday morning Milly was sitting alone having breakfast, for Tom had already gone to work, and Emma was still in bed, when she heard the garden gate open and close. Milly waited expectantly for a knock upon the door, but none came, then she heard the heavy brass flap come down, as something was thrust through the opening, and a letter fell upon the mat.

Milly pushed back her chair, and went to investigate. With a strange feeling of foreboding, tinged with excitement, she bent and picked up the letter. The edge of the contents was showing, for the seal had been broken, and as she turned it over, the reason for this became clear, this letter had been censored by the military!

It was addressed to Mrs.Emma Cartwright. C/o Mr.Tom Laceby. Cottage in grounds of Mount Pleasant. Hull.

Slowly Milly returned to her chair by the table. She listened carefully for any sounds from upstairs, and satisfied that Emma was still sleeping, with trembling fingers and much trepidation, she gingerly extracted the mysterious missive.

Milly opened the single sheet of paper and lay it upon the table. She uttered a low scream and then froze. Much of the contents had been blocked out by the censor, but there was quite sufficient to give Milly a clear understanding of how wrong she and Tom had been, and to realise to what depths her beloved Emma had finally sunk!

For just one brief heart stopping fraction of a second, she experienced a sudden flash back picture of the wicked beautiful Charlotte, her late mistress and the mother of the wayward Emma. Closing her eyes tightly, Milly offered up a silent prayer. *'Dear God, please do not allow the memory of Charlotte, to have this evil influence upon her lovely daughter. All through the life of Emma, I have done my best for her, but it doesn't appear to be enough. Please get her to repent and ask forgiveness.'*

However, there was no reply from this silent room to Milly's heartfelt plea, and with a heavy heart she again read the contents of Emma's letter.

It began. *My darling loving Emma. What a wonderful leave that was. We made such glorious love so many times I completely lost count, and though you came to meet me every day for nine days, never once did you speak, until that last day. Remember what your reply was, when I mentioned if I had left a little Carter behind, that would do as a small deposit towards settling my account with the Cartwright family?*

You laughed and said. That would be just wonderful, and then after giving me one more kiss, you ran off across the fields. I miss you terribly Emma. All my love. Tim.xxxx.

There was much more than that, but it had been entirely blacked out.

With a huge sigh of part frustration and part resignation, Milly folded this all revealing letter, and slowly replaced it in the envelope, wondering what on earth she should do about it. Upon hearing a movement in the bedroom above, denoting the imminent arrival of the subject of her thoughts, Milly quickly hid the offending missive in a fold of her dress.

For several days after Tim's letter had arrived, Milly was still worrying about what she should do with it, she dare not tell Tom, for she knew he would go berserk, and quite probably throw Emma out of the cottage. Then she had an idea, there was one person she could trust above all others.

A late September sun was shining brightly as Rose went to open the door in answer to the bell. She was surprised to see a rather shamefaced Milly standing there.

'Good morning Milly. What can I do for you?' The tone wasn't hard, for Rose had sensed immediately that her visitor had come to offer some kind of olive branch, for she was well aware of the friction that had existed between them of late, and she would do almost anything to alleviate this problem, and return to normal.

Opening the door wide, Rose smiled a welcome. 'Come in my dear. Go and sit in the study while I organize tea.'

Moments later she reappeared carrying a

tray containing a small pot of tea, milk jug, cups, sugar and biscuits. Milly was perched tentatively upon the edge of a chair, looking somewhat like a scared middle aged woman coming for an interview for a position in The Big House.

'Sugar and milk?' Milly nodded. When Rose handed her guest the cup of tea, she noticed Milly was very tense and almost on the verge of tears.

'Now please sit back Milly and enjoy your tea, nothing is as bad as it seems.'

Milly emitted a hollow laugh. 'No? I think even you will begin to doubt that after you have heard what I have to say,' she paused for a moment, searched for a handkerchief, then dabbed her eyes and nose.

'Oh! Rose. Please forgive me for my recent actions. I have no right to come here and burden you with this terrible problem, I feel so ashamed.'

Rose reached over and placed a comforting hand upon the arm of her anguished friend. 'There there Milly, please don't take on so, remember a trouble shared is a trouble halved.'

Without another word, Milly withdrew the somewhat creased letter from a pocket of her dress, and silently handed it to Rose.

No expression of surprise or disgust

disturbed the smooth placid brow of the miller's daughter as she read, and then reread the contents of that mind blowing missive. Slowly she returned the letter to it's rather grubby envelope, and handed it back to Milly, then she stood up, and walking over to the window, she stared out over the Humber in the direction of Watersmeet and her beloved mill, with unseeing eyes.

For the mind of Rose was not on the letter she had just read, nor on the expected baby, not even on Emma. No, the thoughts of the miller's eldest daughter were steeped in memory, the memory of how many times she had upbraided her sister Charlotte on just such occasions as this, and now here she was being dragged through it all again, by the wayward love-child of that same beautiful sister. It seemed as though, even from the grave Charlotte continued to haunt her.

Milly coughed impatiently. 'Haven't you anything to say to these revelations Rose?'

No sign of the anger and tumult raging within, was apparent on the features of Rose, as she turned and faced the worried Milly. 'No, I'm sorry Milly. What can one say? The damage has already been done, and I am afraid we shall just have to live with it. Though knowing Emma's mother as I did, I'm not surprised her daughter allowed Tim

Carter to have his way with her, he wouldn't have found it very difficult I can assure you, and letting herself become pregnant, then this evil charade of not being able to speak, must be some kind of deep laid plan with the ultimate, though hopeless intention of trying to resurrect her marriage.'

Milly stared at her. 'Do you really think that is what this is all about?' she asked, in obvious disbelief. 'Though I must say, over the years Emma has reminded me more and more of her beautiful mother, and I'm afraid in many ways she has followed in the footsteps of Charlotte! There must be something we can do Rose. Can't Charles enquire where Tim Carter is stationed, for according to the letter, he is serving in one of the services?'

So, a disillusioned and unhappy Milly left Mount Pleasant, and though Rose did have a word with Charles that night, nothing came of the many enquiries he made as to the whereabouts of a certain Tim Carter.

Finally at her wit's end, Milly showed the much maligned letter to Emma's father.

For several pulsating minutes Tom sat rooted to his chair, then without warning, he suddenly leapt up, walked swiftly to the foot of the stairs, and bellowed 'EMMA!' at the top of his voice.

A sheepish, now five months pregnant Emma, came slowly down the stairs, finally reaching a chair and lowering herself into it, facing her irate parent.

Tom flung the letter on the table in front of her.

Emma picked it up and commenced reading. No sign of anger, distress or of any interest whatsoever, flickered across her countenance, or even those blank lacklustre eyes. She read it, folded it, and carefully placed it in the envelope, then calmly handed it back to her father.

Tom could hardly contain his anger. 'Haven't you anything to say about this you little slut! Don't give me any more of that can't speak rubbish. I've suspected you all the time, but now we know you're lying. I should have believed that French miss in the first place. According to his letter, you could evidently speak to that bastard Tim Carter. My God! If he ever shows his face around here again, I'll kill him!'

Milly reached over and placed her hand upon his arm, but he roughly thrust her away, and cursing angrily to himself, he marched out of the cottage, slamming the door to behind him.

Though life carried on as normal to outside appearances, inside that cottage the tension was almost unbearable, for Tom would just get up in the mornings, have his breakfast, and without a word to either his wife or his daughter, reach for his cap, and leave. He never returned until the evening, had his tea, then went upstairs, and stayed there until morning, when the whole stupid charade would be repeated.

After a month of this childish behaviour, Milly could stand it no longer, and this particular morning she turned on him. 'I suppose you think it's clever behaving in this manner towards your only daughter. Have you ever thought of how she was conceived? Just try and jog your memory a little, Mr. Tom Laceby. Back to a certain log cabin in a small clearing in Brackley's Wood! Where you seduced the lovely Charlotte, God rest her soul. Just think on, and try to show some sympathy towards this poor girl.'

Tom had visibly winced when Milly had mentioned Charlotte and the log cabin, and though he never uttered a word, that evening when he returned, after the meal he stayed downstairs with his wife and daughter.

The atmosphere in Tom's cottage became a little more bearable after Milly's outburst, and several times he was on the point of apologising for the arrogant way he had behaved, though somehow, he just could not bring himself to do so.

Finally, in February of the following year, Emma's time had come.

The hospitals were so overcrowded with war maimed and wounded, Milly had decided Emma should have her baby at home. The midwife was duly called, and as Emma appeared to be having a difficult time, stayed with her.

For eighteen hours, the once elegant Lady Brackley, struggled, sweated, cursed and screamed, until finally a fine healthy looking baby girl appeared.

At precisely the same moment his daughter entered this world, Tom Carter on board a ship in Mid-Atlantic, left it, for his ship was torpedoed by a lone German submarine, with the loss of all lives!

Meanwhile Emma, because of her previous abortion and a long difficult birth, was hovering very close to death, in fact she passed away when her baby was only about one hour old!

16

Though the war was at last beginning to turn in favour of the Allies, these world shattering events had very little impact upon the residents or estate workers of Mount Pleasant.

For the fact that Emma was now dead, meant they had been left with the distinctly unenviable, and quite huge responsibility of caring for, and bringing up her daughter.

Tom would have absolutely nothing to do with the poor tragically orphaned mite, for he found it quite impossible to forgive his daughter for her adulterous lifestyle, and also for deceiving everyone with her ridiculous voluntary lack of speech.

Milly, who had always been so good with children, yet never ever having one of her own, proved to be completely at a loss as to how to deal with a new born baby.

Therefore Rose had to step in and fill the breach, and after finding a woman who had recently lost her own baby, at least she knew Emma's daughter wouldn't go hungry!

When that particular problem had been solved, she invited Paul and Margurite to go shopping with her into Hull, to buy all the necessary accoutrements a new born baby girl would be likely to need. Rose had not looked forward to that shopping trip, though actually she thoroughly enjoyed every moment of it.

Of course, because of the war, many of the things her and Margurite would have loved to have bought, were unobtainable, so they had to make the best of what they could find.

Nevertheless, when Charles saw the heap of clothes, nappies and even a cot and a pram, piled up in the hall, he gasped in amazement.

'How many babies are we catering for in this establishment, may I ask?' He said, as he walked in upon the apparently happy threesome.

'Hello grandpapa,' they all chorused together, Rose and Margurite collapsing in an untidy heap upon the sofa.

'Only just the one, I hope,' replied Paul

'Oh I don't know,' rejoined a flushed Margurite, smoothing down her crumpled dress. 'I wouldn't mind half-a-dozen, providing they were all as sweet natured and as beautiful, as that little one upstairs.'

Rose smiled secretly to herself, for she had noticed earlier, whilst out shopping, how enthusiastically Margurite had thrown herself into buying baby clothes, and that afternoon a small seed of speculation regarding the future of the new baby, Paul and his French Mistress, had been sown in the assiduous mind of the Miller's eldest daughter!

17

Twelve years had elapsed since the Allies
had declared Victory over the Nazi hoards
in Europe, and demolished the arrogant
German Reich, that Hitler had proudly
proclaimed. *'Will last a Thousand Years!'*

Twelve years that had seen the British
people suffer extraordinary shortages of all
commodities regarded necessary for life in a
civilised community. However, at last the
world suddenly seemed a better place, people
were laughing again, and though much of the
new furniture was Utility, there were sweets,
fruit, and even clothes in the shops!

★ ★ ★

During those years, a great deal had
happened at Mount Pleasant, for soon after
Paul had realised he was a free man,
unencumbered by the chains of wedlock to
the late delectable, unpredictable Emma, he
had proposed and been accepted by the
beautiful Margurite.

Though Margurite loved children, and had
mentioned that fact on more than one

occasion, after several months and much anguished soul searching, it became quite evident that she would never bear any of her own.

The newly married couple had moved into Mount Pleasant, and Margurite couldn't spend enough of her time with Emma's baby daughter. Because of the apparent impossibility of the French Mistress ever becoming pregnant, it was soon realised the perfect solution was at hand!

Consequently, Margurite and Paul adopted the daughter of his late wife. Of course all of this had happened some time ago, and when the adoption was declared official, the joyful parents had taken the child to church, and had her Christened, Charlotte Rose Cartwright!

Though the name was partly the idea of Rose, when she occasionally thought of her late sister Charlotte, she would have doubts about it, but would then comfort herself with the thought. 'That lightening never strikes in the same place twice!'

When Charlotte was old enough, Margurite had registered her as a pupil at The Gables, and during the years she was there, she and a boy pupil had become very close.

They had met on her first day, when she was only five and he was only six, yet the mutual attraction had been instant and was obvious to all. His name was Richard Short, and if it was possible, he would never leave her side either in class, or outdoors.

Some of the other children, particularly the boys, would often tease him, but this never seemed to bother him, for he was a well behaved polite boy, and very popular with pupils and teachers alike.

Except on one occasion, when Richard had reached the age of fourteen. He was a big lad for his age, and had the appearance of eventually becoming quite a tall young man.

However, on this particular afternoon, he had been playing football for the school team, and when the final whistle blew, he rushed off the field searching for his beloved Charlotte. He ran through the sports pavilion and out to the back, calling her name, but she was nowhere to be seen!

Completely baffled by this unprecedented turn of events, Richard paused, and was about to retrace his steps, when he heard a faint cry for help. Tearing round the corner of the building, he almost fell over one of the bigger youths from the sixth form, trying to rip the clothes off the beautiful young Charlotte!

He had her on her back on the ground, and she was fighting and scratching like a wild cat, and then Richard hurled himself forward.

'Get away from her, you filthy scum,' he cried, as he grabbed the youth by his hair, and literally dragged him off the petrified Charlotte.

Not being used to treatment like this from a junior, the older boy sneered, and came at Richard. 'Right, young Short when I've finished with you, you can stay and watch, if you can still see!'

That was the day young Richard Short finally found himself. He had often had the urge to stop this bully, and others of his ilk attacking younger and smaller boys than themselves. However, they had never bothered him, so he had always passed them by, until today!

The love for his beautiful soulmate, provided Richard with super human strength, far beyond his years, and filled with a primeval urge to destroy, he hurled himself at this bully who had dared to interfere with his beloved Charlotte.

The result was spectacular, as this human cannon ball literally pummelled the sixth former to the ground, and silently continued to thrash him, until one of the teachers, aided by several cheering pupils, managed to pull him off, and the disgraced older boy staggered to his feet, and covered in his own blood, beat a shambolic retreat.

Richard shook himself free of the teacher and his admiring class mates, and quickly turned his attention to Charlotte.

She was leaning against the wall of the pavilion, trying to smooth her crumpled dress, and crying quietly to herself. She looked up as he approached. 'Oh! Richard,' she sobbed, flinging her arms around him. 'He was horrible, thank God you came to my rescue, please don't ever leave me dear Richard, I really don't know what I would do without you.'

On that day Richard Short grew up. As he placed his arms around the young delectable Charlotte, and listened to her whisperings of her love for him, he suddenly felt ten feet tall!

'Of course I shall never leave you Charlotte, and don't you worry about the scum who attacked you, he won't bother you again, nor I imagine will anyone else, after the thrashing I gave that one.'

The story of Richard's fight and Charlotte's subsequent remarkable rescue, spread like wildfire throughout the school, resulting in the older pupil being expelled in disgrace, and Richard being hailed as a hero!

This snippet of news worked it's way through the grapevine, eventually being discussed over dinner at Mount Pleasant.

'What's this rumour I hear of you being

attacked by some youth at The Gables, young lady?' asked Paul, as he poured himself another glass of wine.

'It is no rumour darling,' cut in Margurite. 'This horrible youth from the sixth form had Charlotte down upon the grass, and was trying to remove her clothes, when a younger boy who apparently worships the ground Charlotte walks upon, suddenly appeared, and went berserk, almost killing her attacker!'

Paul turned to his lovely adopted daughter. 'Is that true Charlotte? Did this gallant knight of your's almost kill the monster who attacked you?'

Charlotte emitted a sweet girlish laugh. 'No, not quite daddy, though he did give him a thorough good hiding, one he won't forget in a hurry, and yes I'm pleased to say he does appear to worship the ground I walk upon, though that may be a slight exaggeration. However, that young man will not cause me any more trouble, because he has been expelled, and after what Richard did to him, I don't think anyone else dare attack me!'

Charles, who had been listening intently to this conversation, suddenly spoke. 'Richard, you say. Richard who, may I ask?'

Charlotte bestowed a ravishing smile upon her favourite relative. 'Of course you may ask granpapa. In fact I have been longing to tell you all, about Richard for some time. His name is Richard Short, I think his family have something to do with shipping. Anyway, he had been attending The Gables for a year when I started. We met on my first day, and for some reason, even at that early age, the attraction was instant and mutual, and we have been together ever since!'

To everyone's surprise, Charles gave a loud chuckle. 'So, you think his family have something to do with shipping do you?'

Charlotte appeared puzzled. 'Yes,' she replied hesitantly. 'I really don't know why, I think he must have mentioned it sometime.'

Again Charles laughed aloud, then seeing the baffled looks on his companions faces, thought he had better explain. 'Sorry my children,' he began. 'Please forgive the hilarity, but apart from Cartwright's, Short's is the biggest shipbuilders yard, and trawler owner along the river!'

Paul smote the table with his fist. 'Of course! I thought I knew the name. My word young lady, if you manage to stay in touch with your young hero, and their family and ours ever become united. Good Lord, we should be the biggest shipbuilders in England!'

Everyone laughed at Paul's excited comments, everyone that is, except his daughter, and she just smiled quietly to herself.

18

As the years passed, Charlotte became ever more beautiful, looking increasingly more like the other Charlotte, and each night Rose went to bed, she prayed that this lovely sweet natured young woman, would never deign to follow the same wicked path as her late sister!

Charlotte was now twenty-one, and this second week in August had just returned for the last time, from the College for Young Ladies in Switzerland, and tomorrow Richard would be home for good, from Cambridge.

Margurite went with her to Paragon Station to meet Richard's train.

They stood on the platform eagerly scanning the faces of each male passenger as they alighted from their respective coaches, then Charlotte suddenly screamed. 'There he is!'

The two of them dashed forward, cutting a swathe through the oncoming crowd of disembarking passengers. Charlotte, being the younger, was the first to greet him.

Unable to speak, so full of love and emotion, she just flung her arms around his neck, and hugged and kissed him, until finally

Margurite gently moved her aside, and said. 'Steady Charlotte, leave some of him for me.'

That remark broke the ice, and from that moment on, Charlotte never stopped talking.

Richard hadn't failed to notice how his beautiful Charlotte had grown up during the last months, and the following day he tentatively suggested they should walk down to what they called their lakeside love nest! They had spent many idyllic hours in the cottage, but had never actually made love, and today if she agreed, he resolved to put that matter right!

It was a beautiful morning, and Charlotte acquiesced immediately to his suggestion, after making one of her own. Consequently, they didn't walk down to the lake, but went by car, taking plenty of food and drink with them to last the entire day!

Arriving by the lake, they carried the picnic basket, and placed it in the cool of the cottage, then strolled down to the water's edge.

Hanging on to his arm, Charlotte removed her shoes and tentatively placed her dainty toes in the water. 'Oh! Richard, this is beautiful, it's ever so warm, come along and have a paddle.'

With that, she let go of his arm, pulled her dress up round her thighs, and moved further into the lake. After taking only two steps, and emitting a startled scream, she completely disappeared!

Spluttering loudly, but actually laughing, she bobbed up again, and swam to the bank.

Richard offered his hand, and helped her out of the water, and looking decidedly drenched, though apparently enjoying it, she then proceeded to remove her dress.

He looked at her askance. 'Darling. What are you doing?'

She removed her head from inside the wet garment and flung in on the grass. 'Paul darling, if you expect me to wear that dress for the rest of this day, you are sadly mistaken. Now will you please go to the car and bring the towels I put in the boot, Then remove all your clothes, and come with me for a swim. Please!'

While she was speaking, Charlotte had taken off her underclothes, which of course were also dripping wet, and she stood now, her young vibrant, beautiful body as naked as the day she was born!

Richard couldn't move, he was rooted to the spot! He had never before seen a naked woman, and after the initial shock, he rejoiced in the experience, for this glorious body belonged to his darling Charlotte, and for the first time in his life he felt his loins begin to stir!

'Darling, you can see me like this as often as you wish, but please get the towels, and then join me!'

Her words broke in upon his thoughts, and shaking himself back to reality, he tore across the intervening stretch of grass, grabbed the towels and dashed back to the lakeside, ripping off his shirt as he went.

Within two minutes, they were swimming out towards the middle of the lake, both completely naked, their bodies touching as they swam. Though the water was lovely and warm, after about twenty minutes they had both had enough, and swam towards the shore.

Gathering up their clothes and towels, they made a dash for the cottage, and after a thorough rub down with the large bath towels, and their skin literally glowing with good health, Charlotte suddenly pushed Richard down upon the bed.

They were both virgins, because they had each saved themselves for one another, but on that glorious, never to be forgotten day, in this wonderful lover's hideaway by the lake, they really discovered their true destiny, and the meaning of everlasting love.

Friends and relatives of Richard and

Charlotte, people who had grown up with them, and had known them for most of their lives, quickly realised they had never known them at all!

For if they thought the young couple had been in love for many years, that was as nothing to the way they behaved now. Wherever they went, in public or in private, they were always kissing and cuddling, and didn't seem able to leave one another alone!

Because of their obvious deep love for each other, it was formally agreed by their respective parents, that it was time arrangements were being made for the wedding of the year!

However, in this life, it is very rarely everything goes according to plan, yet no-one could possibly have foreseen the terrible events that were about to unfold. That awful fate which had dogged the Cartwright family for so many years, and which everyone thought had died with Thomas Cartwright, or moved on to other pastures, without the slightest warning, suddenly reared it's ugly head again!

Marcia, who had spent most of her life in the nursing profession, only had one more week to go, then she would be retiring, and leaving the life she loved, to enjoy a well earned rest.

She was walking through one of the elderly patients' wards, when a nurse called her name. 'Sister Teesdale, can you please spare a moment?'

When Marcia had retraced her steps and satisfied the requirements of the young nurse, she was about to turn away, when an old lady spoke to her. 'Excuse me sister. Before you married, was your name Marcia Cartwright!'

Intrigued, Marcia moved to the old lady's bedside. 'Yes, my dear, it was. Why do you ask?'

'Because, many years ago, I knew a young lady by the name of Emma Cartwright, and she told me about you!'

Now more deeply interested, Marcia moved closer, and drew up a chair. 'Please tell me, how did you come to meet Emma?'

The old lady coughed, took a sip of water, and struggled to continue. *It was, maybe a couple of months after she had her baby!*

Marcia, suddenly startled rigid, interrupted. 'After she'd had her baby! What baby?' The look upon her face, and the tone of her voice, obviously upset the old lady, for she sank lower into the bed, and tried to pull the bedclothes higher up, to almost cover her.

Marcia immediately realised her very unprofessional mistake, and endeavoured to console the patient. 'Extremely sorry my dear, I never meant to cause you any distress, but you must realise, this matter is very important to me, for you see, I never knew Emma had a baby. Was the baby a boy or a girl? And how did you become involved?'

Her informant appeared sad and rather wistful, and she faltered a little when she spoke. 'We were living in the same block, and had become firm friends. Anyway, it was one night during one of those very bad air raids, she asked me to take her baby down to the shelter, and said she would follow later. Well shortly after we got in the shelter, this massive bomb hit our block, and completely demolished it, killing Emma and everyone else who had stayed inside.'

For a long moment Marcia remained silent, thinking furiously. Finally she spoke. 'What happened to the baby?' she asked anxiously. 'Did he or she survive?'

'Oh yes. The baby was a boy, well of course I couldn't manage to bring him up alone, so when I realised his mother must have been killed during that terrible air raid, *I took him along to the Orphanage!*'

The old lady's last words were no more than a whisper, and Marcia realised she was very tired, and that all this talking had been too much for her, so after thanking her for this very important information, she decided to leave.

Marcia couldn't get home fast enough that evening, and when she finally arrived, she dashed down the hall, and bursting with excitement, thrust open the door of the dining room.

The family were seated around the table having dinner, and all heads turned in her direction, as the conversation ceased.

Before Marcia regained sufficient breath to say anything, Charles spoke. 'I say my girl, that's no way to enter the dining room, when we are having dinner. And you're late,' he added sternly.

Marcia, still flushed and excited, replied. 'I know, I know, sorry daddy, but just wait until I tell you the wonderful news I have heard today,' she paused, and looking round at her eager captive audience, she took a deep breath and continued.

'Today, I met an old lady at the hospital, and she told me an incredible story. Apparently she lived in the same block as Emma during the war, and on the night of that very bad raid, when Paul found her in the street suffering from shock, she had left her baby boy with this old lady to take down to the air raid shelter, and said she would join her later. Well the old lady thinks Emma was killed, but of course we know different.'

Again she paused for breath, and when no-one spoke, they all appeared to be struck dumb by these totally unexpected revelations from the past, Marcia continued.

'However, the best news is, the baby survived, and unable to care for him herself, this lady took him to the Orphanage!'

It was at that moment, all thought of dinner completely forgotten, that everyone began speaking at once.

'Orphanage!' Rose cried. 'Does that mean he may have been adopted by someone?'

'Do you mean a son of mine, could be in an Orphanage?' shouted Paul.

Charles could see this family gathering was getting a little out of hand, and to try to bring some semblance of order to the excited gathering, he thumped the table with his fist. 'Now please be quiet! There is no point in everyone shouting at one another in this unseemly manner. We must find out from the authorities if this boy has been adopted, and if so, by whom. Also what his name is.'

'I will do that,' said Marcia. 'I have certain connections at City Hall through being a nursing sister at the hospital, and I think I know just the person who will be willing and able to help us.'

★ ★ ★

So it was agreed, though the following day being a Saturday, no-one was available at City Hall, therefore the family had to endure an agonizing wait, until Monday.

Saturday however, turned out to be a glorious day, much too fine and warm to stay indoors, so Charlotte and Richard decided to take the car, and indulge in another picnic by the lake.

They again swam naked, and then sunbathed on the soft grass, and they were lying face down upon towels, allowing the hot sun to caress their naked bodies, when suddenly, a voice they both recognized, said quietly. 'I say, just come and see what I've found!'

Richard immediately leapt to his feet, struggling, though not very successfully to drag his towel up with him, in an endeavour to hide the lower part of his body, as Eric Teesdale walked up to stand beside his wife.

'Well it really is amazing what gets washed up by the tide these days,' he said facetiously, whilst drinking in the soft contours of Charlotte's exquisite, delicately tanned young body.

Marcia noticed her husband's intent stare, and taking his arm, she said. 'Yes, it is rather,

250

though I think it might be better for you my lad, and probably me, if we were to walk a while, and maybe look the other way!'

Up to that point Charlotte hadn't moved or taken any part in the conversation, now however, she raised her head, and turned to look at them. 'Oh! Don't worry so Marcia,' she said laughingly. 'If Eric enjoys looking, don't spoil it for him.' Whereupon, she stood up, and facing them, nonchalantly lifted the towel, slowly draping it around her shoulders!

Richard stared at her aghast. 'I say darling, please try and show a little more restraint, we don't want your relatives to think the worst.'

'Dear Richard, I think most of them realise by now, that you and I know what life is all about, and that we don't come down here just to have a picnic!' Then flinging her towel to the ground, she turned and ran down to the lake. 'Come along Richard, let's have one more swim before lunch.'

He looked appealingly at the two spell-bound spectators, and then not knowing what else to say in this bizarre situation, which was entirely foreign to him. 'Care to join us?' he joked weakly, as he followed his beloved Charlotte into the all welcoming embrace of the cooling waters of the lake.

When they had finally finished their swim, and walked up to the cottage, Marcia and her husband had departed. 'Do you think Marcia will say anything to your folks about us darling?' Richard asked, frowning slightly, as he wondered what the repercussions would be, if she did.

Charlotte turned and looked at him. 'No Richard of course not. For Heaven's sake get rid of that silly frown. What's it matter if she does? We're both adults, dash it all, we shall be married in another month! Now come here and kiss me.'

So the two clung together, their wet naked bodies glistening in the brilliant sun, and they kissed wildly, passionately, before going once more into their private paradise, to again slake their mutual sexual appetites.

★　★　★

On the Monday morning following that incident by the lake, Marcia paid a visit to see her friend at City Hall, and though she couldn't discover any factual information just then, concerning the adoption of Emma's baby, her friend's answer was that she would set the wheels in motion and contact Marcia as soon as possible.

Approximately one week later, a rather important looking letter arrived at Mount Pleasant, addressed to Mrs.Marcia Teesdale.

Marcia, having finished going to the hospital every day, was of course at home when the mail came, and with trembling fingers she ripped open the envelope, for City Hall was stamped upon the back, and she suspected this was the reply the whole family were waiting for.

She was correct, only this wasn't quite what any of them had expected, or desired!

Marcia read the contents once, and in stunned disbelief, read the letter again, then uttering a faint cry, she collapsed and slumped to the floor, the letter fluttering down beside her.

Rose, upon hearing a peculiar sound, went to investigate, and seeing the prostrate figure of Marcia, urgently called the maid. Finally the two of them managed to half carry, half drag the inert body through to the study, and gently lower her on to a chair.

While the maid dashed off to the kitchen for a glass of water, Rose slowly passed a bottle of smelling salts beneath the nose of Marcia.

Suddenly, she jumped violently, almost knocking the bottle from Rose's hand. 'What happened? Where am I?' she asked, her eyes staring and rolling wildly.

Rose reached out and touched her arm. 'Steady my dear, for some reason you fainted, but everything is alright now. I really don't know what caused you to faint, but it seemed to be just after the postman called.'

Immediately Rose finished speaking, Marcia seemed to miraculously recover her senses and her memory. 'Yes! Oh! Yes, that was it! The letter. Where's the letter?' she asked, frantically looking round the room. 'I received a reply from City Hall. Where is it?' She was almost screaming now.

Rose offered her a drink of water, but she roughly pushed it aside. 'No! I must find that letter. Maybe I dropped it in the hall.'

'I will go and have a look,' said the maid. A moment later she returned, the missing letter in her hand.

'Thank you,' cried Marcia, snatching the missive from her.

'What does the letter say my dear?' asked Rose quietly, as she reached forward to take it.

'I really don't think you should know mother, the result of the contents are too dreadful to contemplate.'

Still the hand stayed outstretched. 'Marcia, please. I'm waiting. This is something that concerns all the family.'

Slowly, and obviously regretfully, the dutiful daughter passed the extraordinary, mind numbing contents of this ghost from the past to her mother.

Rose sat perfectly still, as though cast in stone. Her expression didn't change, she never uttered a sound, and even gave no indication that she had finished reading, until she slowly began to fold the letter, before handing it back to Marcia.

'Well, what are we going to do now?' asked her daughter.

Rose looked at her, then allowed her gaze to linger a moment on the rapt intent expression upon the face of the maid, for she knew the girl would be hanging on to every facet of their conversation. 'I think it is time for tea and biscuits, please attend to it,' she said sweetly.

After she had left the room. 'You know better than to ask questions concerning the family, in front of the staff Marcia.'

'Yes mother, I do. I'm awfully sorry, but you see, you have no idea how much this letter has upset me, or what a terrible effect the result will have upon the people concerned!'

They decided to say no more about the matter until Paul and Margurite, Charles, Charlotte and Richard, also Eric, Marcia's husband, were all sitting down after dinner that evening. In the meantime, Rose had informed a stunned Charles of the much maligned

255

letter, and had been most impressed by his stoical acceptance of the contents, muttering something about. *'That old Cartwright curse, coming back to haunt us from the grave!'*

The family were all sitting comfortably, some reading, others just talking, yet there was an inexplicable almost tangible atmosphere of impending tragedy in the room, everyone could sense it. Somehow the feeling must have emanated from one or all of the three people who were aware of the contents of the letter, and become unknowingly transmitted to other members of the family.

Earlier it had been agreed that Marcia should be the one to open the proceedings, and divulge the contents of the reply to her enquiry from City Hall, for after all, the letter was addressed to her.

To bring her audience to attention, Marcia tapped on the table with her fingers. Everyone immediately stopped whatever they had been doing, and looked up in eager anticipation.

'I can tell you are all expecting to be told something rather momentous tonight. Well I can truthfully say you will not be disappointed. Sorry, that was the wrong word to use. I'm afraid you will all be very disappointed, some more than others. As you are all aware, I discovered through sheer coincidence, that Emma, Paul's late wife had a child who survived those dreadful air raids, was taken to the Orphanage, and subsequently adopted. I then asked a friend at City Hall, if she could help me to trace the child, and possibly discover his or her whereabouts at the present time, and this is the reply I received.'

Marcia then removed the letter from it's envelope, and in complete silence, spread it out upon her knee, and commenced to read.

'Dear Marcia. I managed to discover the whereabouts of the late Emma Cartwright's child. He is a boy, and was Christened Richard Cartwright. On his birth certificate, the name of Paul Cartwright is given as the father. When Mrs. Cartwright was reported missing, he was taken to the Orphanage just as you were informed, and from there was later adopted by a Mr. and Mrs. Short! A year after the adoption his name was changed, and he now has the name of Richard Short!'

A low cry of utter desolation from Charlotte, mingled with gasps of disbelief from other members of the family, prevented Marcia reading any further. However it wasn't necessary, for all the relevant facts had been disclosed in those first few horrific lines, and now the whole Cartwright family were on their feet, trying to comfort a terribly distraught Charlotte and Richard.

Amidst the mayhem, caused by everyone giving advice in the strongest possible terms, Richard placed his arm around the sobbing Charlotte, and said quietly. 'Please come with me darling, and please don't cry, everything is going to be alright!' He then helped her to the door, and without a single member of the family so much as giving a glance in their direction, the two slipped through, and ran down the hall together hand in hand, then out into the welcome, all enveloping darkness of the night.

★　★　★

Marcia led the way, she had a suspicion where the two lovers might be. All the family and several of the estate workers had been searching most of the night, and now as dawn was breaking over the placid waters of the lake, Marcia called out. 'I can see Paul's car!'

In all there were about a dozen people in this particular party, including Rose, who in spite of her age was determined to do everything she could to help. They all rushed down towards the car, then suddenly, still about ten paces distant, came to an abrupt halt.

A piece of hose pipe was leading from the exhaust, through a small aperture in the floor of the car!

Dreading the worst, Marcia moved swiftly forward, the others following in her wake. *Two naked bodies lay upon the rear seat, entwined in a lover's embrace!*

'No! No!' Screamed Marcia, as she pulled frantically upon the car door handle, but the car had been locked on the inside!

Tom Laceby, who was also in this party, picked up a large stone and smashed a window on the driver's side, enabling him to open the door. He glanced at the petrol gauge, the ignition was still switched on, and the tank was empty!

He leaned over and released the lock on the rear door, then stepped in and covered the two inert bodies with their own clothes.

'Come along Marcia,' he said quietly, as he held her arm and led her gently away from that macabre scene.

★   ★   ★

There were a few members of Charlotte's close circle of friends, who suspected she hadn't always been telling the truth, when professing her virginity, and saying she was saving herself for Richard. These suspicions were verified when the report on the post mortem became public knowledge.

For the report not only stated that they had both died as a result of carbon monoxide poisoning. *It also said, the young lady was three months pregnant!*

Epilogue

Rose smiled wistfully at her friend Alice, as they placed fresh flowers upon the newly formed grave of her beloved Charles.

The scandal and publicity, with more than a whiff of incest, which had surrounded the affairs of the Cartwright family, since the inquest on the deaths of Richard and Charlotte, had proved too much for the failing health of Charles Cartwright, and very soon after that horrendous event, he had passed away peacefully, one night in his sleep.

Though Rose was nursing a broken heart, everyone was amazed at her fortitude, as she adhered to her late husband's wishes to the letter, having his body brought to his beloved village, and buried in the cemetery, where he first met his 'Beautiful Cemetery girl, with hair the colour of ripened corn.'

It was whilst Rose was visiting her old friend Alice, after the funeral, and after Alice had told her of a very nice bungalow that was for sale, built on the hill top, with a wonderful view overlooking the confluence of The Three Rivers, and only a short distance from The Maze, where Charles had knocked down Halle all those years ago, that she had suddenly decided to return to Watersmeet, and spend the rest of her declining years among the familier scenes of her childhood.

Rose and Charles had been contemplating this move for some time, because Mount Pleasant was far too big for them, even with the younger people living there. Then the scandal that had besmirched the name of Cartwright, and the death of her husband following so quickly afterwards, had caused her to think more seriously about leaving Hull, consequently when Alice told her of this bungalow, she had immediately bought it, and set the wheels in motion for her return.

As these two old friends walked through the cemetery gates and out on to the road, Rose suddenly turned left, and proceeded to walk along a path running alongside the cemetery wall.

'Where are you going dear?' Alice called after her. The Miller's Daughter stopped, and a single tear ploughed a furrow down the lines of her face, as she remembered a tall broad shouldered young man, asking her that very same question many years ago, and as she turned and looked back at the cemetery, she raised her head, and murmured. *'Thank you Charles for a truly wonderful life!'*

Later that afternoon, as these two old friends were sitting on a seat by the maze, discussing times long gone, Alice turned to her companion.

'You know all about your ancestors on the Cartwright side of the family, don't you dear?'

★ ★ ★

Rose looked puzzled. 'No, I wouldn't say I know everything about them, what have you in mind Alice?'

Her friend leaned closer, in a conspiratorial manner. 'Of course you know about Thomas Cartwright losing his wife and children, in an horrific explosion on board his ship, 'The Elisabeth Kate' moored by the river bank just down there.' Alice raised her arm and pointed with a finger.

'Well, the locals do say, that on a clear night in deep mid-winter, when there is a full moon, and the earth is sleeping beneath a white protective blanket of sparkling frozen snow, the ghostly figure of a tall fair haired woman has been seen, moving slowly along the foreshore, leading a young child with each hand! I have never seen her myself, but that is what the people of this

village say, and she is the reason Thomas Cartwright spent so many years at the window, in that room at the top of High House, searching for his beautiful long lost wife and children!'

Dear Reader.

According to Legend, many years ago, a captain sailed his ship up The River Humber with his new bride on board, and anchored by the foreshore immediately below a village named Alkborough. {Watersmeet}

This village is situated in North Lincolnshire and is built on an escarpment overlooking the confluence of three rivers. The Humber, The Ouse and The Trent. The captain came ashore and made his way up to the village, to replenish his supplies. Whilst there, a terrible storm ensued, during which he lost his bride and his ship!

Later, the captain returned to the village and built a tall three storey house, which to this day is often referred to as The Captain's House, or High House. From a window in a room at the top, he could look down upon the resting place of everything he held dear.

That is The Legend. The Cartwright Saga, is my interpretation of that Legend. I hope you enjoyed.

The Author.

Taken From

Lyrics Of Lovely Lincolnshire

Watersmeet
(Alkboro Hills)

I must be back on Alkboro Hills
When violets come again
When cushioned banks of primroses
Are smiling through the rain
Beneath a latticed canopy
Of fine old English trees
When 'Lords and Ladies' wake anew
To greet the springtime breeze.

And I would walk the sylvan glades
Of witching Walcot Wood
Where beech and elm through centuries
The scourge of time have stood
My laggard steps renewed would trace
The maze called 'Julian's Bower'
Where childhood steps have stumbled on
Through many a jocund hour.

O let me tread the cowslip meads
That lie so cool and sweet
Where Humber, Ouse and silvery Trent
Join hands at Watersmeet;
Where brown sailed barges homeward glide
On tides that never cease.
O then, my 'wildered wanderlust'
Shall find the pools of peace.

By
Edith Spilman Dudley

We do hope that you have enjoyed reading this large print book.

Did you know that all of our titles are available for purchase?

We publish a wide range of high quality large print books including:
Romances, Mysteries, Classics
General Fiction
Non Fiction and Westerns

Special interest titles available in large print are:
The Little Oxford Dictionary
Music Book
Song Book
Hymn Book
Service Book

Also available from us courtesy of Oxford University Press:
Young Readers' Dictionary
(large print edition)
Young Readers' Thesaurus
(large print edition)

For further information or a free brochure, please contact us at:
Ulverscroft Large Print Books Ltd.,
The Green, Bradgate Road, Anstey,
Leicester, LE7 7FU, England.
Tel: (00 44) 0116 236 4325
Fax: (00 44) 0116 234 0205

STRANGER IN THE PLACE

Anne Doughty

Elizabeth Stewart, a Belfast student and only daughter of hardline Protestant parents, sets out on a study visit to the remote west coast of Ireland. Delighted as she is by the beauty of her new surroundings and the small community which welcomes her, she soon discovers she has more to learn than the details of the old country way of life. She comes to reappraise so much that is slighted and dismissed by her family — not least in regard to herself. But it is her relationship with a much older, Catholic man, Patrick Delargy, which compels her to decide what kind of life she really wants.

DUMMY HAND

Susan Moody

When Cassie Swann is knocked off her bike on a quiet country road, the driver leaves her unconscious and bleeding at the roadside. A man later walks into a police station and confesses, and they gratefully close the case. But something about this guilt-induced confession doesn't smell right, and Cassie's relentless suitor Charlie Quartermain cannot resist doing a little detective work. When a young student at Oxford is found brutally murdered, Charlie begins to suspect that the two incidents are somehow connected. Can he save Cassie from another 'accident' — this time a fatal one?

SHOT IN THE DARK

Annie Ross

When an elderly nun is raped and murdered at a drop-in centre for drug addicts, the police decide it's a burglary gone wrong. Television director Bel Carson sees pictures of the body, and is convinced that this was a ritualistic murder, carried out by a sadistic and calculating killer. Then he strikes closer to home, and Bel determines to track him down. As she closes in on the monster, she senses that someone is spying on her home. And, in a final, terrifying twist, she finds herself caught in the killer's trap . . .

SAFFRON'S WAR

Frederick E. Smith

Corporal Alan Saffron, ex-aircrew, is desperate to get back into action, but instead he's posted to Cape Town as an instructor, along with Ken Bickers, a friend about as hazardous as an enemy sniper, who considers Saffron a jonah for trouble. Within half an hour of arrival, Saffron's jonah strikes, and he makes an enemy of Warrant Officer Kruger, who turns Saffron's cushy posting into total warfare. With recruits as wild as Hottentots, obsolete aircraft, and Cape Town's infamous watch dog, Nuisance, Saffron's sojourn in South Africa becomes a mixture of adventure, danger and pure hilarity . . .

THE DEVIL'S BRIDE

Penelope Stratton

Lord Rupert Glennister's luck at cards and his tireless sexual appetites were thought to be the work of satanic forces. An outraged society made him an outcast until he could redeem himself by marrying a woman of virtue. Calvina Bracewell was a parson's daughter but was bullied into servitude by her 'benefactors'. Rescued by Lord Rupert, she found herself agreeing to his shocking demand that they should marry that very night. For a while, Calvina was happy but then attempts on her life began. Only one man could want her dead, and that was the husband she'd grown to love.